HEAD OVER HEELS

Recent Titles by Judith Cutler

COMING ALIVE *
DYING BY DEGREES
DYING TO SCORE
POWER GAMES
STAYING POWER

* available from Severn House

HEAD OVER HEELS

Judith Cutler

This first world edition published in Great Britain 2001 by
SEVERN HOUSE PUBLISHERS LTD of
9–15 High Street, Sutton, Surrey SM1 1DF.
This first world edition published in the USA 2001 by
SEVERN HOUSE PUBLISHERS INC of
595 Madison Avenue, New York, N.Y. 10022.

British Library Cataloguing in Publication Data

Cutler, Judith
   Head over heels
   1. School principals – England – Devon – Fiction
   2. Love stories
   I. Title
   823.9'14 [F]

ISBN 0-7278-5768-1

Typeset by Palimpsest Book Production Ltd.,
Polmont, Stirlingshire, Scotland.
Printed and bound in Great Britain by
MPG Books Ltd., Bodmin, Cornwall.

For B and F

One

B eth Holyoake leaned her forehead against the window and watched the last of the teachers leave the staff car park. An hour earlier, it had been the Ofsted inspectors making their exit, and she'd twiddled her fingers at them in an ironic wave. Too bad if any of them had seen – they'd as good as written their report and it would be too late to change it now.

She turned back to her desk. So it was all over for another four years. Now all she wanted was to collapse into a hot bath. There was the drive home first, of course: should she take the coast road or the fast dual carriageway which took her past the edge of Haldon Moor? The sight of the broad river meeting the sea or the sound of the wind whistling through the broom? Because, on an evening like this, she'd stop for a few moments to enjoy one or the other – to sweep away the day's problems. One of which – oh, dear – was that the contractors still hadn't arrived to clean the windows. She made a note to get on to the caretaker. Not that he'd do anything, not without a lot of nagging. Jeff Bromwich did nothing without a lot of nagging. He'd seen head teachers come and go and was clearly determined to outstay each last one. Oh yes, by sheer inertia.

There was a knock at her door.

'Come in.' She hoped she managed to put more enthusiasm into her voice than she felt. The inspection had been exhausting for them all. But she must remember that it was the teachers, poor things, who'd had the most stress – their classrooms invaded by experts whose sole aim in

1

life had seemed to be to nit-pick. 'Jane! You should have left ages ago! What about picking up Tessa?' Single mothers didn't have the possible luxury of staying on as long as the work took.

'She's at the homework club,' Jane said. 'I wanted to see that the service engineer did a halfway decent job repairing the photocopier,' she added. She pushed the door shut. It opened again. Another job on Jeff's list. Request number seventeen?

Beth grinned: if Jeff Bromwich was a nightmare, Jane was every head's dream of a secretary – early forties, neat, bright, unflappable. Beth could imagine her, arms akimbo, standing over the poor engineer and reminding him how many times he'd been out to the school this month, with so little effect.

'Did he? Or did he at least get it working?'

Jane shook her head grimly. 'Says we need some new part or other. Need a new machine, if you ask me. I've damned near worn a path traipsing down to that newsagent's – all that stuff we needed for the inspection, and our machine croaking every other day. Did the inspectors really need all that paperwork?'

Beth shrugged. 'All I know is that for the cost of the paper we could have employed half a teacher for at least six weeks. Still, all over now.'

'Mr Starling's outside, wanting to congratulate you on doing so well.' Jane raised an ironic eyebrow, bright eyes sparkling over her specs. 'I told him you were just leaving, but he said it would only take a minute.'

The consolation was that the rush hour would be over before Beth set out.

'How kind of him,' she said. 'Show him in.' But she didn't sit down. She'd make it clear she was ready to leave. She could almost smell the lavender oil she'd use in her bath, almost feel the hot water easing away the stress of the last weeks. In the meantime, however, she must make herself agreeable – Christopher Starling was the Chair of the school governors, and a man not lightly to be offended. Not that she wished to offend him. On the contrary, she was always conscious of how much she owed him: of all those on the panel which had interviewed her, he had been her main supporter, and had continued to back her strongly since. But no matter how grateful she might be, tonight she just wanted to go home.

'Elizabeth!' Starling strode into the room, closing the door, which sprang open again. (While he was about it, Jeff Bromwich could screw her nameplate on straight. She didn't care for a drooping *Dr Holyoake*.) 'Many congratulations! A first-class review!'

'Don't congratulate me,' she said, smiling nonetheless. 'Congratulate the teachers. It's they who—'

'Good workers are nothing without good management,' he said, his smile showing attractive crows' feet and splendid teeth. 'Surely a little celebration . . .'

'I've already celebrated,' she said. 'Champagne for all the staff.'

His eyes widened.

'We keep them back after school for enough meetings,' she said. 'It was nice to be able to give them something pleasant to stay for. Not enough to break any drink-drive laws. But enough to say thank you.' There'd been canapés and other nibbles, and a smile of congratulation for each teacher, and for the support staff too. Not, of course, that Jeff Bromwich had deserved his smile. Or his bubbly.

Starling nodded his approval. 'Your man-management's always excellent. Always.' His smile slipped from officially approving to something more intimate. 'And how are *you* proposing to celebrate? Do I take it from that suit that you're going out? I hope you don't mind my saying how delightful you look in it.'

How irritating if she started to blush. 'A bit of kidology for the inspectors,' she said. 'Blinding them if not with science then with a fuchsia skirt.' If it hadn't impressed them it had made her feel good, anyway. Even in the sales the suit had been at the top end of her budget. But it was so beautifully cut and the colour so flattering to her fair skin and hair, she didn't regret a penny of it.

'And your celebration?' he pursued.

'Three aspirins, for a start,' she said. 'And then an evening with no files.' She patted a pile on the corner of the desk. 'They can look at me as balefully as they like, but they won't get any attention till tomorrow.'

'Aspirins?' He frowned with concern.

'To get rid of the pain in the neck that the inspection's been. And, to be honest, to clear a headache that's been lurking all week. It's been a tough time for everyone.'

'Even for the governors,' he agreed. 'I never realised they inspected us, too.'

'Sometimes,' she said, 'you think they check all the things they don't need to, and don't even look at the things they do. Still, that's inspectors for you.' She snapped her briefcase shut, and shrugged into her jacket. She wasn't exactly leaping up and down like a year eight pupil demanding to be let out, but surely he could see it was time to go.

He looked at his watch.

She fished her car-keys from her bag.

She knew what he wanted, all right. He wanted to ask her out. And it would be fine if he did. She might even accept. Why not? They were both unattached. Even if he was an inch or so shorter than she was, there was no doubt he was good-looking, and if his hair was greying at the temples, that was supposed to make a man look more distinguished, wasn't it? He carried no more than a few pounds more than he should. Altogether he was quite attractive for his age: somewhere, she thought, in his mid-forties. She could always check on his file if she felt it really mattered. If.

But she didn't want him to ask her for a drink tonight. Now it was all over, she was beginning to feel a bit middle-aged herself. Her neck and shoulders were stiff, and her shoes felt uncomfortably full of foot. Middle-aged! She could still claim to be thirty-something! Well, just. She pulled her tummy in: there, that was better. She managed another smile. So long as he didn't take it as a smile of invitation.

'I was wondering,' he began.

Oh dear: he had done.

But he was unexpectedly diffident. He cleared his throat. 'I was wondering whether you'd planned to go to the concert in the Cathedral this weekend.'

'The Bournemouth Sinfonietta?' Talk about finding her Achilles heel: she'd been intending to get a ticket but in the rush of the last weeks hadn't got round to it.

'That's right. A friend of mine has offered me a couple of tickets. I was wondering – would you care to join me?'

'I'd love to,' she said. And meant it.

Particularly as it meant she was free now. As they left the building together, she breathed in deeply. No, not to smell the sea, that would come later. Just to clear her lungs of all the school smells: food and polish and hot young bodies. And something else, she never knew quite what. Maybe Jeff Bromwich bought cans of it, and sprayed the place before even she arrived.

Noticing, Christopher smiled. 'I'm afraid the pollution keeps getting worse – Exeter smells more like Birmingham or Leeds every day. And the traffic . . .' He came to a halt beside her car.

'I can definitely smell the spring,' she countered. 'And listen – you can hear the birdsong even this close to the city centre.'

'You're obviously a romantic,' he said, watching as she let herself in and fastened her seat belt before moving across to his own car. Perhaps it was a criticism, not a compliment: he was off in a spurt of gravel before she'd even gunned her engine.

In the end she chose the coast road. As late as this, there wouldn't be too much traffic. And she even took the long way round, the minor road running between the

Powderham estate and the Exe estuary. She parked in her usual lay-by. Should she walk back by the footpath along the embankment? She might see nests and baby birds. Dusk was deepening and she was yawning: tonight she'd just watch the yachts and dinghies tacking backwards and forwards across the river and listen to the slap of rigging against mast from the boats moored nearby. How many times had she and Richard come in, soaked to the skin? No, best not to think of Richard. She should have taken the A380 instead, shouldn't she? But it wasn't a mere glimpse of open spaces she wanted: it was a day, a whole day, roaming them. Saturday: she'd make that her day for a walk on Dartmoor. Weather permitting, of course. Hell and damnation! Saturday was now Starling day. Another talking, smiling day, when what she wanted was – mentally she dropped her voice into a sexy contralto – to be alone.

At least she could find that at home.

Home, with a glass of wine on her patio, even if she had to sling a rug round her shoulders to keep out the wind. And then her bath, and then – yes, a take-away curry. And early to bed. After all, it would be business as usual tomorrow.

She stowed the car, slung her case on to the hall table, and headed for the wine she'd left chilling in the fridge. It was only as she opened the patio door that she noticed the little red light on her answerphone, flashing peremptorily.

Conrad covered his ears, rubbing the lobes. The wind up here was cold enough to hurt. But he'd stay a few moments longer, before heading back to the Range Rover. Yes, now the last week's low cloud had cleared, you could see as far as the coast. How many miles was it, Hay Tor to the Exe estuary, which was where that golden thread of sea must be? Conrad turned slowly. There might be no living soul in sight, but he didn't feel alone. He felt surrounded by people. History – he was standing on the granite of some old railway – and prehistory – he'd passed hut circles on his way up here. Yes: the sea and the sky and the moor.

He had everything. He smiled as he huddled deeper into the fleece of his jacket. Everything before you'd even clocked your big four-o.

A spiteful gust rocked him. Yes, it was bloody cold. Why hang about here when there was a roaring fire waiting for him when he got home to Tucker's Hay, not to mention discreet central heating? Before they'd left for their cottage in the village, Terry would have selected a bottle of something that would suit Marie's wonderful meal – she'd said something about a goulash tonight. He had a pile of CDs, videos and books to work through. Even the TV. So why – despite the streaming eyes and nose and blue fingers – didn't he make a move? Come on, the light would be going soon. A wild place like this you had to make sure you didn't twist your ankle in some damned rabbit hole. Even someone young and fit could die of exposure during a night in the open at this time of year.

Conrad turned at last, striding out till he came to the shelter of the Range Rover. As he fumbled his keys from his pocket, he took one last look round, and a hard, sharp penny sank.

He didn't want to go home, did he?

Two

B other the answerphone. Beth would have her drink first.
She'd earned it, for heaven's sake. Christopher Starling
had been right: she'd put at least as much into the inspection
as the teachers – the planning, the allocation of resources, the
support. When had she last had an evening to call her own,
let alone a weekend? Now she was at home, confronted by
the face in the mirror, she could admit it: despite the silk
shirt, despite the elegant suit, despite the expensive hair-cut
and make-up, she looked what she felt – tired, tired, tired.

And she still had to go and get her take-away. Much as
she longed for that bath, she'd better postpone it till she'd
eaten. Then she could collapse straight from bath to bed.

She sank on to the patio seat, angled to catch the last
rays of the summer sun. Except, of course, that it wasn't
summer. It was late March, and the sun was way below the
horizon. Across the estuary in Exmouth they might still have
a glimmer. Here in Dawlish it was cool dusk, getting colder.
Chilled white wine indeed! A mug of tea to wrap her hands
round would have made more sense. But she huddled on,
swathed in the rug she'd had the sense to bring out. The
birds were managing a late burst of song. She could just
make out the daffodils glimmering pale under the hedge.
But sitting-out weather it wasn't.

The trouble was, she never knew when to give up, did
she? Shaking her head, she gathered herself up and headed
for the next item on her agenda: food. While she was eating,
she'd think about Christopher Starling and his invitation.
She ought to work up some enthusiasm – after all, she'd

8

wanted to go to the concert anyway, and he was a personable enough man. Much more 'suitable' than Richard.

So why didn't she do as she'd promised herself, take home a chicken Korai and a fluffy naan bread to pig into in the privacy of her kitchen? Because the waiters at the Indian restaurant knew her and welcomed her to her usual table as soon as she stepped inside? And because her favourite beer and a plate of poppadoms materialised as soon as she'd unbuttoned her coat? Or because Carol and Frank from the delicatessen brought their coffee over to her table and sat down to talk amateur dramatics? 'When will you be back?' they wanted to know. The players needed her administrative gifts. 'Any moment now,' she told them, 'now Ofsted's over.'

It could have been any or none or all of those factors. Secretly, she suspected, it was none of them. She dawdled along the Lawn, an area of grass – just that – a tiny park bordered on one side by the main shopping street, on the other by a stream always called the Brook. Eventually she stopped to feed the naan she'd not managed to finish to some ducks still on patrol.

'Why don't I want to go home?' she asked them. 'It's that answerphone, isn't it? I'm scared someone will be summoning me back to school.'

The consensus amongst the ducks, and a couple of the town's black swans who'd casually joined them, was that she was right. She flung them the last crumbs and set off up the hill to the cul-de-sac she lived in.

It was a steep walk and left her embarrassingly puffed. That was something else she'd missed recently – exercise. The same must be true for all of the staff, come to think of it. She ought to do something about that. After all, the school had sporting facilities – not as many as her predecessor had had, the one the governors had persuaded to sell half the playing fields to raise money for the new languages block. But enough for a few people to play badminton or netball at the end of the day. Why on earth hadn't she thought of it before, as soon as Ken, her deputy, had had his heart attack? My God, she'd missed him these last few weeks.

Right. The phone. At least she could use it in the comfort of the living room, her shoes kicked off and her feet up on the sofa.

Bathos. Anticlimax. Nothing to get het up about at all. The message was simply to contact her elder brother, Russell. They didn't see much of each other, these days, and they'd certainly never been particularly close. Beth had been known to refer to him to her very dearest friends – though certainly not within earshot of any of her pupils – as a pompous old bore. Occasionally – and regrettably – she'd vary the description: *boring old fart*. In fact, the adjective *old* was certainly unfair: he was only eight years older than she was. And he was kind and thoughtful, often unexpectedly generous. It was just that he took himself and his needs so seriously. If he'd had the good sense to marry someone to laugh him out of his worries, he'd probably have been much happier. As it was, Sylvia took them more seriously than he did himself, and any residual sense of humour had long since withered on the vine.

It was Sylvia who took her call. 'We'd quite given you up,' she said. 'Russell's phoned you two or three times.'

'I was out,' Beth said, unnecessarily.

'Oh, you and your meetings,' Sylvia said, as if they were some weakness Beth indulged in that she could give up if only she really wanted to.

'That's what a head does – she goes to meetings,' Beth said. Why didn't she simply say she'd been out for a meal? Why not admit to one evening's self-indulgence?

'He was quite worried when you didn't ring back.'

That was what answerphones were for, wasn't it? To collect messages till you had a chance to phone back. Beth bit her lip. Best to keep sarcasm for those who really deserved it – like some of the fair damsels of year ten.

'I'm fine,' she said. 'How are you both? And Emma!' Drat, she should have phoned over the weekend to ask about Emma, and she'd clean forgotten. The poor kid, her only niece, was laid low by glandular fever. Beth had sent flowers and – now Emma felt up to eating again – chocolates and Devon clotted cream. But she hadn't been meticulous in family phone-calls.

'I'm not my usual self, I have to admit. All this nursing on top of the Change.'

Nursing? That must refer to ministering to Emma's needs: Sylvia had never seen fit to earn a living. Spending money might be Sylvia's responsibility, but earning it was Russell's.

Beth responded to her demand for pity with a sympathetic noise: a bracing suggestion about HRT might, in the circumstances, not come well. 'And Russell?' she prompted.

'It's Russell I wanted to talk to you about,' Sylvia said, dropping her voice to a confiding monotone. 'Stress,' she said. 'Stress. All this worry about Emma, you see. At his age – it isn't good for him.'

'Of course not. What's he doing about it?' Whatever it was, Beth hoped it would involve sensible exercise, not just a faddy diet. Russell had been on some sort of diet as long as she could remember, but he'd never lost more than a few pounds, and none of them for more than a few weeks. When they'd made their inevitable return, they'd tended to bring a couple of friends to stay with them.

'What I want is to take him on a bit of a break. A little holiday. Just the two of us. A city break,' she added dourly. As if a month in the Tuscan countryside was what she'd *really* needed. As if their actual destination wasn't worth mentioning.

Beth knew where this was leading. Slowly and inexorably it was leading to the point where she simply had to ask about Emma. Was she going too? Was she well enough to leave on her own? That sort of question. The first had of course been answered already. Which meant that the only contender was the second. And she had a dreadful feeling she knew precisely what the answer would be. Emma had spent many a summer holiday week with Auntie Beth – everyone knew what long holidays teachers had.

Pulling a face at herself in the wall-mirror, she asked a slightly different question. 'So Emma's well enough to go back to work?'

'Oh, no. Not yet. But you see, that nice Dr Grafton thought she might benefit from some nice sea air. So bracing.'

Should she surrender now, or make Sylvia play one more point? Knowing it was in vain, she asked, 'Where were you thinking of?'

She might as well have saved her breath.

'Why, Dawlish, of course.' Sylvia might have been speaking to a dim three-year-old. 'Where else?'

Beth could have told her. Whatever claims Dawlish might have to fame, being bracing wasn't one of them. For some reason, it was the opposite – visitors came, and lolled around all day yawning. She'd done it herself till she'd got used to it – something to do with the little town being damp, and facing away from the brisk – and bracing – westerly wind. But then, lolling around all day was all you could do after glandular fever.

Beth said neutrally, 'It's not Easter for a couple of weeks yet. You know in term time I'm out all day and most evenings too. She may be very lonely.'

'But you must know lots of young people,' Sylvia objected. 'You're a headmistress, after all.'

'I'm not sure any of my pupils would regard going out with the Head's niece as a specially attractive proposition,' Beth observed. No, neither girls nor boys. 'And they live in Exeter, not Dawlish. Ten or twelve miles away.'

'Oh, well . . .'

Beth could see that being wafted away as the most minor of considerations. If she wasn't terribly careful, she'd find herself elected chief chauffeur. And since, to get her day's work done, she rose at six each morning, the prospect of bringing a teenager home with the milk was not at all appealing. Not at all possible, now she came to think of it. She sought for a clinching argument. 'They'd be too young for her, anyway. The oldest is sixteen. I don't have a sixth form, remember.'

Sylvia side-stepped the issue. 'She won't be there long enough to get lonely.'

Ah! 'How long,' Beth asked, 'would you want her to stay?'

'We'll bring her tomorrow afternoon, shall we? Then we can pop off to Gatwick . . .'

'"Pop"? It's quite a way from here. Not all motorway either. Besides which—'

'Well, it had better be the morning then. We'll be down about—'

'Hang on. It's school tomorrow.'

'But surely you can take a couple of hours off! It isn't as if you were a real teacher . . .'

No indeed! 'I'm afraid time off isn't an option. Not with a diary like mine. The best thing you can do is stop off at the school and collect my spare keys – it'll only add half an hour to your journey if you come off the M5 at Junction 30. Oh, bring some milk and something for her lunch – my cupboard's quite bare . . .'

It was only as she put the phone down that she realised how completely she'd been out-played. She might know when Emma was coming: she'd no idea when she'd be going home.

It hadn't been goulash simmering in Conrad's oven, but a pork-and-cider casserole, with slices of apple melting into the rich gravy. Baked potatoes. Carrots and broccoli cut up small enough for him to steam in five minutes. Everything was organic, even the pork, from one of the tenant farmers he'd acquired when he'd bought the estate. In the fridge, cider from Dan Huntspill's farm down the road, white wine and Perrier. Just for good measure, a bottle of red on the shelf near the Aga. Yes, they looked after him, Terry and

Marie. Too well. If he wasn't careful she'd simply sling out the baked potatoes he couldn't manage to eat. Well, they might make a welcome addition to the compost heap, or even a treat for Falstaff, down in his sty, but they'd make a good potato salad for tomorrow's lunch – recycling food was something he'd got in the habit of doing when he was a student.

He stared at the casserole. Yes, it still got to him, from time to time, not completing his course. Oh, dropping out of uni had been the only sensible thing to do at the time – even his dad had said that when he'd seen the recording contract – but it had left him feeling, well, sort of unfinished. As if, despite all he'd done in the music business since, he'd never quite lived up to his potential.

Potential? Potential for becoming a teacher or something, and living in a semi in Salisbury? Conrad looked around the kitchen. What about Tucker's Hay? Wasn't that actual? Real and actual?

He ladled the casserole on to a plate, adding vegetables. He'd eat in the kitchen, of course – he'd at last cured Marie of laying a solemn place for one in the oak-panelled dining room – and drink cider. He spread the paper where he could read it while he ate. His mother would have boxed his ears for him, seeing him slum like that. But it kept his mind off the silence that somehow the radio or TV never quite defeated. Like all his neighbours, he took the *Western Morning News*. He read that with his mid-morning coffee. What he saved till the evening was the *Guardian*, which had usually arrived minus at least one section. Since it came by van over five miles of ill-maintained road, he could scarcely send the lad back for the rest of it. What was he missing today? No, it was all here. He scanned page upon depressing page of international news, before moving on to home-grown misery. There was a whole-page piece on British inner-city kids growing up in poverty. Christ, what a life! He'd never known anything like that – not him, from his safe suburban home.

He turned the page. Sports news. And there wasn't much comfort in that.

On impulse, he slung on a jacket and grabbed the potatoes and a few carrots. How about an apple, too?

'Falstaff! Falstaff! I know you're asleep but you're never one to turn your snout up at an apple.'

There was barely enough light from the house for man and pig to see each other, but Falstaff shoved a bleary head under Conrad's hand.

'I was bored, you see, mate. God, sorry about that pun. No offence, eh?'

Falstaff swallowed any hurt pride with the apple.

Conrad scratched the ear presented to him. 'I'll have a word with Marie about those Golden Delicious, shall I? Tell her you prefer Braeburn?'

Falstaff grunted.

'You got anything to report, then?'

Falstaff made it clear it was time for bed. So Conrad trailed back to the house. Perhaps he might have an apple too.

So that was that. Emma was coming tomorrow, going whenever. Since there'd be no time in the morning, Beth had better sort out the spare bedroom for her now. Bed-linen, towels. A run round with the duster and vacuum cleaner wouldn't come amiss. And the bathroom – that was missing Mrs Marsh. But her sciatica was nearly better, she assured Beth. She'd be back in a week or so.

Beth was reaching the vacuum cleaner from its cupboard when she looked at her watch. No, she'd never yet spring-cleaned at night. And she wasn't about to start now. Was she?

She was. But not immediately. Funny how the more you needed sleep, the less it came and the less it stayed with you. If you wouldn't take pills – and Beth certainly wouldn't – how could you deal with those blank, sleepless hours? Pulling herself up on her elbow to check the time

15

– nearly three – she remembered that spare room and its patina of dust. Well, she thought, swathing herself in her dressing gown, at least cleaning might be more productive than the committee papers that were her usual small-hours diversion. But all the dusting and vacuuming couldn't blank out the question that buzzed in her head: how had it come about that she, whose whole life was devoted to out-manoeuvring other people, should always succumb to her sister-in-law's wiles?

The peace and quiet of the country, indeed! Conrad prowled round, listening to the creaks and groans as Tucker's Hay settled down for the night. There was no way he'd be sleeping for an hour or two yet. He stared at himself in a mirror. Old and losing its silver it might be; it still showed up the deepening bags under his eyes, the almost permanent frown lines between his eyebrows. He was developing a stoop, too – all those hours hunched over the computer.

What about a walk? It was a lovely fine night.

If it had been too dangerous for him to walk at dusk, it was a bloody sight more dangerous now. On impulse, he pulled on jeans and heavy sweater. One advantage in having no neighbours was that there was no one to disturb if he got the car out and took to the hills for a bit.

In the event, he found himself heading south. He'd always been a sucker for moonlight over the sea. OK, he'd have to put up with stars tonight, but they were very bright. He'd pick up the Teignmouth road at Newton Abbot and go right along the coast to Exeter. There were a couple of places to stop: an official lay-by overlooking the Teign estuary and Shaldon, and another – unofficial – in a lane on the outskirts of Dawlish. Someone had erected a huge cross at the top of the hill to celebrate the Millennium. It was still floodlit. From the road near the base was another view he always found touching – the little town cupped in the deep valley, quietly asleep. Like Bethlehem in the carol, he supposed.

Tonight, however, someone was as sleepless as he – in

an isolated house on the far side of the town lights came on, went off, as someone moved from room to room. Poor bugger.

Conrad got back into the Range Rover: home with the heater on and a tape for company. He checked through the pile in the glove-box. How about something comforting like Judi Dench reading *Silas Marner* . . . ?

Three

Emma stared silently out of the car window. Countryside everywhere. It wasn't even pretty countryside, just some great fat pigs on a hillside near the motorway. Oh, there'd been that orange camel a few miles back, and ever since Mum and Dad had been wittering on about some grey elephant in another field nearby. She hadn't seen it. God knew what the camel and elephant were made of. God knew why anyone should want to make huge models of animals just to stick them in some field. God knew why her parents kept rabbiting on about them.

'Distracting, that's what. A danger to motorists. They should never have got planning permission for something like that!'

On and on they went. As if it mattered. And every so often, Mum turned round to ask what she thought, and every time she said she couldn't care less Mum asked about her temperature and her glands. As if they cared. Leaving her stuck in Dawlish while they were off enjoying themselves in Rome. Dawlish! With an aunt! As if she was a kid again.

Actually, Beth wasn't so bad, not really. She'd given her some OK times when she was a kid, and she always came up with something cool for birthdays and Christmas. But she wouldn't be there most of the time, and even if she was, who, for God's sake, wanted to stay with a headmistress?

'Do stop chewing your hair, dear.' Oh God, didn't Mum *ever* stop nagging?

'Look, the weather's picking up!' Dad said.

Yes, that really mattered, didn't it! As if she was going

to get her little bucket and spade and play on the beach. Not that there was much else to do. No pier. No clothes shops. No cinema. No McDonald's. No clubs.

A real hole.

And Beth would no doubt be telling her all about the ducklings they'd got in the hatchery by that stream-thing in the middle of the village – really major news, that. Yawn, yawn.

'Tired? Why don't you try and have a little nap, dear?'

Which was about the most sensible thing Mum had said today. Perhaps if she went to sleep she might wake up to find it had all been a nightmare, and she was back at work, smiling at that new security guy. The one with the nice bum . . .

This was one of those days when you sat and stared at the phone and willed it to ring. Who the hell had said it was a good idea to write music straight on to computer?

Conrad sat back and had another go at willing the phone. No good. No new e-mail in the system, either. Back to the main screen.

He stretched, looking around him. Yes, the place looked good. Not like when he'd bought it. He'd been so angry that people before him had let it go so badly. Leaking roof, dodgy foundations, rising damp, dry rot – he'd had the lot. That panelling over there . . . He got up to have a closer look. Some of it had been so badly damaged by rot and woodworm, there'd been no chance of rescuing it, so he'd brought in a team of craftsmen to do it up. He stroked some of the panels: yes, they'd done a great job. Texture and colour – you could hardly tell the new from the old. And where they'd knocked two small rooms into one decent-sized one, they'd patched the plasterwork so no one could see. He touched it with the tip of his finger.

Come on: back to work.

On his way back to his desk, he diverted to the window. Not a great view from this one. They'd built the house in a

19

hollow to shelter it from the worst of the wind, those early wool workers. So there were only a few rooms from which you could see anything except rising slopes of gorse, heather and bracken. Oh, and the odd sheep. If you went to the front of the house – and he couldn't stop himself doing just that! – then you could see the vast acreage of Dartmoor. He stood at the open front door, and breathed in deeply. What now? A coffee, and some of Marie's latest batch of biscuits? A stroll down to discuss life with Falstaff?

'Come on – they're good for you, fresh carrots. Help you see in the dark.'

Falstaff eyed him but consented to eat the carrot.

'I know, I know. I should be working. But sometimes you work and work at the stuff on screen, and the more you work, the less it makes sense.' He ran his hands through his hair. 'You see, I've always thought up the tunes, and then written them down longhand. Takes ages. Then you've got to put in the accompaniment – all the harmonies, and so on. More ages. So what I'm trying to do is type the stuff straight on to the computer, which does all the rest automatically.'

Falstaff snuffled for another carrot.

'I'm supposed to be working on a new album, see. No distractions. And since I bought Tucker's Hay because the poor place was desperate to be put back on its feet, it makes sense to do it here. Oh, and it's nice to have you to talk to.'

Falstaff nodded in acknowledgement.

'So shall I stick with the computer or go and write down this tune that's coming in my head?'

Falstaff retired to his scrape for a roll in the mud.

Conrad turned slowly . . . Yes! By the time he'd got back to his music room and his guitar, the melody was ready-formed in his head. Yes. Easier to play and then write it down. Damn the bloody computer! Yes. Here it came . . .

Marie had to call him to lunch three times before he even registered her presence.

How many New Initiatives could a single government minister invent, for goodness' sake? Beth dropped the last thick wad of paperwork on top of the others and sat down, head in hands. Just when she'd thought she'd got the job licked, just when the school had come out with an exceptionally fine report, there was a whole new set of criteria by which it would now be judged. She might as well take up a new hobby – running up a down escalator.

She checked through the diary. There was half an hour before the next meeting – to discuss with the Head of Science a maternity-leave replacement for a Biology teacher. If only Helen could have cloned herself – imagine, a ready-made teacher as good as her mother! Meanwhile, time for her stroll.

With nine hundred on the roll, the school was too large for her to know every pupil. It had been bad enough learning all the staff members' names. But she certainly knew all the problem kids, and, moreover, where to find them. Which meant, of course, not in the class where they were supposed to be.

Old joke or not, the cycle shed was just one likely refuge.

The trouble was, Beth had made a rod for her own back. Given the perennial problems of school buses and ferrying parents, one of Beth's first moves had been to bring in RoSPA and the local police to organise a massive cycle-awareness campaign. Every child in the school who could ride already had been trained; and all the non-riders had been given as much help as possible. There'd been sponsorship drives for helmets and bright-wear. The media had outflanked a rampant parent-car lobby and provided positive support. So now King's Barton was very much a school on wheels. Hence the cycle shed's continued existence.

And continued existence as a trysting place and smoking area.

Before she could even check for cigarette ends, however, a bell rang. Not the discreet end-of-lesson chirrup. A full-scale, alarming ring.

Beth did what was strictly forbidden to any pupil in a fire-drill. She kicked up her heels and sprinted back to the building.

They were at it again, only this time Emma did feel like joining in. She'd woken up in the car in some suburban road, desperate for a pee, with her parents gone off God knew where.

At last they'd come back, Mum as usual walking slightly ahead, and turning back to wag her finger at Dad, as if he was in it again. And Dad had pulled his hand from his trousers pocket and looked at his watch at least twice in the walk back from the school entrance. Look at him: sports jacket, flannels – and he was going to Italy in that gear!

'Typical. Just typical,' Mum was saying, as she got back into the car. 'How are you, dear? Not too cold?'

Quite warm, actually, with the sun shining on the car. She'd had to open a window and slip off her coat. 'Where on earth have you been?'

'Ask your dad. It's his sister, not mine.'

'Well? Dad?'

'She can't help being busy, love.'

God! He sounded just like a sheep.

'She may not be able to help being busy, but there's such a thing as common courtesy. We've got a plane to catch, for goodness' sake. And here's Emma, frozen with cold.'

'But—'

'A sick child, and she keeps us hanging about all that time. Do stop chewing your hair, dear.'

'Her secretary said it was an emergency.'

'Keeping us out in the playground—'

'What sort of emergency?' Emma asked.

'Three fire engines. A couple of police cars,' her father said.

'One of the kids messing round. Smashing the fire alarm,' Sylvia threw over her shoulder. 'So the whole school had to traipse out and hang around waiting. And we were kept out while the firemen checked.'

'One of them was certainly a woman,' Russell said, as if he approved.

'A woman? In all that silly gear? Yuck, that's really gross.' She supposed that if you were a great beefy woman with spots there might be some point playing boys' games, but not if you had a nice figure and a complexion like hers. This wretched illness had taken off a few pounds, but that was all to the good. She was through to the regional finals of the Face of Young Britain already – and she couldn't imagine there'd be too much competition from women used to shinning up those ladders. 'Anyway,' she asked, 'have we got the keys?'

'Yes. And the burglar-alarm code. And the central-heating instructions and everything Beth thought we'd need,' Russell added.

'Except Her Ladyship's own presence. Well. What are we waiting for? Come on, Russell. We're supposed to be catching a plane – remember?'

One of these days he'd have to find out about birds. Conrad snorted. Not a lot he didn't know about birds! All the screaming, all the touching. All the bedding, come to think of it. He sat on a granite outcrop and tried to remember how many women he'd been to bed with since he'd been a star. Gave up. Tried to work out how many women he'd been to bed with since he was twenty-five. OK. Since he was thirty.

Which was, of course, how he'd come to give up women.

Not, he admitted, on a permanent basis. And there were times when this celibacy business was a bit of a pain. It wasn't as if there weren't a couple of really nice women, both of whom had been steady friends in his life when he'd needed friends, and who were ready to share his bed because

– yes – they loved him. Both of them. And he loved them. Both of them. He could have lived with either of them. At which point his father had taken him out to the garage to tinker with the lawnmower and had said, 'It's not a matter of who you could live with. It's a matter of who you can't live without.'

The bird he was watching now was some sort of hawk, he supposed. It was hovering, wings almost unmoving except for caresses from the very tips, fixed on something far below. All around, the moors and their inhabitants went about their business. A cluster of ponies harassed some tourists. A van dispensed ice cream. Sheep munched steadily.

The bird dropped.

It didn't rise.

There was one fewer inhabitant of the moor to go about its business.

At least Beth had phoned Emma to warn her that she'd be late. Did that give her the excuse to stop on the way home, in the lay-by she'd chosen last night? Too bad, for the moment, if it didn't. This time she locked the car, slipped on the walking shoes she always kept in the boot, and headed along the footpath that lay between the railway and the estuary. Just for five minutes.

Out on the river, three dinghies in succession were flipped over by the wind. She grinned – what would Richard have said? She squared her shoulders resolutely. No. She mustn't look back. The trouble was, all she had to look forward to was her first evening with her niece.

Emma had lost a lot of weight: Beth could see that. But she'd acquired a woman's figure – nothing of the half-child about her now. Look at those facial bones. And her skin. Her complexion might be a bit muddy after her illness, but there wasn't a sign of a spot, past or present. A few days of sea air and good food and she'd be truly lovely.

Good food? Despite her efforts with herbs and cream,

the chicken Beth had cooked had largely languished on the girl's plate. Emma had managed to nibble a couple of sautéed potatoes, but had done no more than shunt round her plate the local purple sprouting broccoli and early carrots. The white wine was clearly too dry for Emma's taste – but then, Beth wasn't sure if glandular fever and alcohol mixed. At last Beth had found some Devon ice cream lurking in the depths of her freezer: that had gone down well.

Seven forty-seven. So what about the rest of the evening? Would Emma expect to be entertained? Beth hoped not, not with the amount of work she'd got to get through, simply to catch up with what she should have done at school. Not to mention her usual evening's load.

And if she did, how would Beth go about it? She didn't see Emma as a likely opponent in a needle game of Scrabble. Nor would she imagine her settling down to watch the sort of video that lurked at the bottom of Beth's bookshelves. Come to think of it, most of them had been Richard's choice, and rather too grim even for Beth. Tomorrow she must send Emma off to the video store – always assuming the poor child, already yawning her head off, could walk so far.

'What would you like to do now, love?' Beth asked. She couldn't get her tone quite right – it veered between the cooingly tender, possibly appropriate to a real, suffering, bed-bound invalid, and the bracing tone she tended to adopt to girls whose period pains coincided with Maths tests.

Emma shrugged. 'Watch telly, I suppose.'

How a daughter of Sylvia's came to be allowed to use the word *telly* Beth couldn't imagine. But it went with the Estuary English that Emma favoured – like so many of Beth's own pupils, whose Devon burr it did little to improve.

'OK. Find your way about with the zapper – I'll just load the dishwasher. Tea or coffee?'

Emma flapped a hand. 'Whatever.'

What an evening! None of her mates phoning: not long-distance, not to a mobile. She couldn't be bothered to find her personal stereo. It'd be somewhere in her bedroom. *Her* bedroom. She didn't think so. It was all pastel walls and no posters. It was like being in hospital. She might go to bed soon. When she'd got the energy to move. Meanwhile, there was nothing but the telly.

Nothing worth watching on that, of course. And there was Beth, over in the furthest corner of the room pretending she was watching it too, but all the time shuffling through papers she kept dragging out of her briefcase.

God, how much longer could she stand this?

Four

'Someone's trying to catch your eye,' Christopher said, taking Beth by the elbow to steer her through the mêlée of concert-goers leaving the Cathedral.

'Really? Where?' Despite the pressure of his hand, she stopped to look round.

'That man over there. With the glasses and grey hair.'

'Where? – oh, it's a friend of a friend of mine.' She waved back. 'Toby Field,' she added parenthetically. But that was all. Christopher didn't need to know that Toby was the long-term partner of Mike Becks, her Head of Languages. She had a feeling that for all his enthusiastic support of equal-opportunities training, Christopher was not going to be keen on gay relationships. On the other hand, some men she'd been out with wouldn't have drawn to her attention the fact that another man was waving at her, so the points remained balanced.

Toby mimed a telephone call: it wasn't clear who was supposed to call whom, but she smiled and moved on.

'Now,' Christopher said, coming to a halt at the edge of the cathedral close, 'may I suggest supper to round off a very pleasant evening?'

Huddling into her coat against the wind, she shook her head. 'I'd love to but I've already eaten—'

'A drink, then,' he urged.

It was hard to refuse without being churlish. 'I'd love to. But—'

'Not another but!' He might have been laughing, but she sensed offence.

'But my niece is staying with me.'

'Your niece?'

'She's been very ill with glandular fever, and now her father's not very well, either,' she said, though on reflection she thought he had looked as fit as he ever did. 'And her parents thought a rest down here might do her good.'

He shot her a hard but not unkind look. 'And who else in your family is in need of a rest? I hate to say it, Elizabeth, but you have been looking – shall we say, jaded?'

'I'm surprised I'm not looking like a half-embalmed corpse after these last few weeks. To be honest with you, Christopher, I don't know what to do with her. Emma, that is.'

'"Do with her"? You shouldn't be doing anything with her, Elizabeth. When you're at home, you should be able to relax!' He smiled at her, head slightly on one side. 'Any woman working as hard as you do needs to be looked after, not to be the one doing the looking.'

She smiled. It was strange to have a little sympathy and understanding coming in her direction rather than going from her to others. She did what she hadn't meant to do, in case he misunderstood the invitation. 'I feel I've got to get back home to keep an eye on her. But there's no reason why I can't offer you a drink or a coffee there. If Dawlish isn't too far out of your way.' Perhaps it would be. Perhaps she hoped it would be.

Exeter to Dawlish and back to his home in Topsham: a round trip of some twenty miles, simply for a coffee. Christopher might well want more, mightn't he? She checked in her rear-view mirror. Yes, his BMW was still following her. Not that he could have got lost: the little towns were studded along the main coast road, and it was simply a matter of driving in a straightish line till you hit Dawlish. And although her house was tucked away in its quiet cul-de-sac, her sketch map would guide him should he lose her in the narrow streets.

Beth wasn't at all sure she wanted him to have more. Not yet. She liked him. Yes, she certainly liked him. But could she ever do more than like him?

One thing was certain: to go to bed with a man, she had to do more than like him. So she'd have to make sure, right from the moment he arrived, that he knew that sex was not currently on the agenda.

There: she'd allowed herself to do it again. *Not yet. Currently.* Sooner or later she'd have to know what game she was playing so she had at least some idea of its rules.

One rule she'd always had. A no-smoking rule. And it was obvious, as she opened the front door, that someone wasn't observing it.

Now, however, with Christopher parking neatly in the drive behind her car, wasn't the moment to tackle Emma.

'Hello! I'm home!' she called.

There was a muffled reply – not from Emma's bedroom but from the living room. Beth swore under her breath. She'd never for one moment imagined that Emma would still be up: the last couple of evenings had seen her in bed by nine thirty. So where could she put Christopher? In the living room with Emma and the television? She would have to insist on it being switched off, but in effect that would be to send Emma to bed, separating her from whatever film she happened to be watching. Not desirable in terms of tantrum potential. So what could she do? Though she was proud of her kitchen, it was a kitchen for cooking, not entertaining. She'd have to let him into her study, wouldn't she?

'What a delightful room,' Christopher said, taking the tray from her as she appeared at the top of the circular staircase. 'Where shall I put this?'

'Just here.' She pushed a small table between the two easy chairs that occupied one end of her loft conversion. 'Thanks. This is decaffeinated – I hope you don't mind, but at this time of night—'

'Not at all. I'm trying to cut down anyway. I've even wondered about decaffeinated tea . . .'

So Beth had got herself a bloke, had she? Emma stubbed her cigarette out on the saucer she'd found in a cupboard. Fancy Beth having no ashtrays. And fancy Beth taking the bloke upstairs. Except that, of course, upstairs was only that study of hers, the one she and Dad had had rows about, because he'd said she was making improvements that wouldn't repay her when she sold the place. She'd not been up there yet herself. Well, not a lot of point, really. Just books, Beth said. So why had she taken the bloke up there? Why hadn't she brought him in here? It would have been nice to see another human being, after being cooped up in here all evening.

Tipping the ash into the kitchen bin – well, most of it: some went on the lid, and a little on the floor – she wondered, now what? A glass of milk and some biscuits. She took them into her bedroom.

She'd better draw the curtains. As she did so, she looked out – couldn't see much, of course, with the light on. So she switched it off and looked again, slopping the milk. Now that was something like a car. A Beamer! Fancy Beth managing to pull a bloke with a Beamer! Perhaps after all it was too early to be lying down. Maybe she should have a look at him: quite casually, of course.

Conrad let himself into the Range Rover. It had been a good evening, though he wished he'd booked early enough to avoid having to spend the time staring at a pillar. Still, that was what you got with church performances: bad sight lines and dodgy acoustics. They said the University concert hall was better. He'd better get some bumf: find out when their next concert was. People never believed him when he said he liked classical music. They forgot that music had been part of his degree, forgot that even to be a pop musician you needed to know some nuts and bolts and how to fit them together. Fortunately they'd also forgotten that his first live performance had been at Lettie and Chaz Wood's wedding singing 'Hear my Prayer'. He couldn't have been more than eight, that pie-crust frill under his chin making him look as innocent as if he hadn't sloshed some of his dad's duty-free vodka into the communion wine.

He chuckled. But as he pulled away into the traffic, he found himself sighing. It would have been so good to have someone to chew the whole thing over with. The 'Andante' in the Mozart concerto – the pianist had been downright vulgar, the way he'd pulled the melody around. He'd felt like standing up and offering to play it himself.

He'd looked around during the interval for someone to natter to. But everyone had seemed to be part of a couple, and the best he had managed was to smile at some old biddy who was fixing her hearing aid. But who else might he have wanted to smile at? The leggy blonde who'd sat in front of him and nodded all the way through, clearly trying to show the world how musical she was? Pity she'd been off-beat almost all the time. Or that couple who, from their nudges and stares, had clearly recognised him? No, he'd simply looked through them. It was either that or point out it was a night off for him. Well, a whole year off. And his time off was private time. Of course, there was the small matter of that concert in the States . . .

Which way home? Should he burn some rubber on the motorway-standard A38 or pootle all the way along the coast road? Even as he sat tapping his fingers on the wheel, he knew which it had to be. He fished in the glove-box for the Dictaphone he always carried and sang into it as he went. He had an idea he was in for a night tapping the new melody into his computer – let it see what harmonies it might come up with. The A38 it would be.

Beth had to admit that nothing could have been more neutral than Christopher's conversation – ostensibly. They'd talked uninterrupted school for twenty minutes now. But somehow he managed to turn each comment into a compliment to

her. She felt more and more uncomfortable. She could have
parried personal praise, patted compliments back to him if
she'd felt like it. But it was hard to fend off professional
flattery, which is what it was. Or was he the sort of man
who found it hard to express feelings? She knew nothing
about him, not the real Christopher as opposed to the public
one. At the moment she was too weary to redirect the
conversation back to him. And half her mind was worrying
about manoeuvring him downstairs and out of the bungalow
without his noticing the only flaw in the loft conversion: the
fact that the lovely staircase rose from the corner of her
bedroom. Carrying up the coffee tray, she'd been all too
aware of the clutter on her dressing table, and the duvet's
blowsy droop to the floor. She'd have to remember to keep
the bedroom as immaculate as the living room as long as
the latter was occupied by Emma.

At last, she did what she'd been trying hard not to do all
evening. She yawned. A real gaper. They both laughed, but
again she sensed that he was offended. Christopher Starling
was clearly a man for good manners.

'I'm so sorry . . . it's—'

'It's the end of a difficult week,' he said, forbearingly.
'I hope that that fire-alarm business was a one-off, by
the way.'

'I shall do my best to ensure it was. It's usually some
hapless child wanting to postpone a test. We have ways of
finding out,' she added.

'I'm sure you have. And I'm sure you'll deal adequately
with the culprit,' he said kindly. Suddenly he looked at his
watch, expressing surprise and rising to his feet. 'Goodness
me! I'd no idea it was so late. And I have to be up betimes
tomorrow.'

'On a Sunday?'

'I'm a sidesman. Eight o'clock communion service. I
can't let people down.'

He led the way down, while she carried the tray and
doused lights. So she didn't see the expression on his face

as he froze abruptly in the doorway to the hall. Stepping sideways, she managed to see what had stopped him in his tracks.

'This is Emma, my niece,' she announced, managing to keep her voice steady. 'Emma, this is a friend of mine, Mr Starling.'

Well, the girl remembered her manners – so well that Beth was convinced that the meeting in the hall had not been as accidental as the girl's dishabille suggested. She smiled and stepped forward to shake Starling's hand.

He responded, but turned to Beth immediately. 'As I was saying, an early night is called for. Thank you for your company, and for your kind hospitality. Goodnight, Emma.' Stepping past her, he opened the front door himself.

Beth followed. Hugging herself against the chill – surely they couldn't be having a frost at this time of year? – she asked, 'Shall I see you out? The drive's very narrow – I want to get the gateway widened.'

'But you'll get cold.'

She shrugged.

'In that case I'd be very grateful. And I was very grateful for your company tonight. It was nice not to be an old widower huddled up to the fire.' He turned and took her hand. 'Thank you,' he added, kissing her cheek.

She watched him out of sight, despite the cold. What had either of them got from the evening? A little company? Fair enough. But why had he made that detour simply to down one cup of coffee with her? If a man were besotted, twenty miles was nothing. But he wasn't besotted, any more than she was. Was he? Could he somehow have been appraising her and her home? That was what it felt like. But it didn't make sense.

Meanwhile, what on earth could she say to Emma? Something light about house rules, perhaps – she could touch on the smoking and maybe not make too much of the fact that Emma had presented herself to her guest wearing nothing but a low-cut T-shirt.

But Emma's door was firmly shut, and no light shone under it. Balked, Beth stalked off to load the coffee things into the dishwasher. To find – occupying, as well it might, pride of place – an eighteenth-century Spode saucer, covered with tobacco burns. Oh dear. This low-key talk about house rules was going to get heavy, wasn't it?

Emma knew how it would be. Beth would switch on that smile – the 'I-am-your-kind-and-understanding-aunt' smile – and then start on her. Beth didn't nag, so much as reproach, rather like Dad. And Beth reproached *herself* – 'I should have explained this at the start . . .' She had, of course. She'd said when they'd all come down to see her soon after she'd got the job that the place was a no-smoking zone. Yes, but that had been because she was trying to get that sexy bloke out of her hair. The one that smoked like a chimney. Richard – that was the one. What a looker he'd been. Emma moved under the bedclothes: she hadn't half fancied him, and she was pretty sure he'd fancied her, too. Why didn't Beth have any photos of him anywhere? She hadn't found one, not even in Beth's bedroom.

So what was the best way of avoiding one of Beth's sermons? Lying here pretending to be asleep had only bought her time. She needed a strategy.

Beth couldn't believe her ears. Emma, shopping-mall addict, asking for a run in the country?

'It would be quite a nice day for it,' she'd replied. 'And we could find a pub for lunch. If you're sure it wouldn't tire you?'

'Be great, wouldn't it? See a few sheep and things.'

Beth nodded. 'Which would you prefer: the sea or the moors?'

'There's quite a lot of sea round here,' Emma observed. 'How about a few moors? And, do you know, I reckon I could manage a bit more breakfast. Got any eggs?'

While she beat the eggs – fresh and organic from the

greengrocer on Queen Street – into a frothy scramble, Beth considered. When should she tackle Emma about the house rules? No time was a good time. But she knew that when you were sharing a house you couldn't put off things like that lest they fester. As she tipped the eggs into the pan, she began, 'Emma, I should have explained this at the start . . .'

Well, she'd get a new dressing gown out of it, that was one thing, Emma supposed. She'd expected the lecture about the smoking, of course, but then Beth had found other things to moan about. The saucer turned out to be some antique worth an arm and a leg, not that anyone could have known. And then Beth had started on at her for embarrassing her guest. Embarrassing him! Not bloody likely. The old stoat had been turned on, hadn't he? Well, not exactly turned on, but interested. Not that Emma would have looked at him. And she was surprised Beth had: the guy was going to be quite gross soon – fat, grey-haired, and short enough for Beth to look down on his bald spot.

'But I've never needed a dressing gown before,' Emma said, wide-eyed. 'You know, with my bathroom at home being en suite.'

Beth had raised one eyebrow. God, that was how she kept all those kids in order, was it? Emma found herself shifting in her seat as Beth turned back to the stove.

'There. Scrambled eggs. Another slice of toast? And tomorrow, if I have time, I'll pop into Marks and Spencer to get you a dressing gown, shall I?'

Emma started on the eggs. She'd never really understood that saying about discretion and valour, but she suddenly realised it had something to do with sitting down and shutting up.

Five

C onrad perched on his rock at the foot of the Tor and stared at the Sunday invaders. Grockles – that was what the natives called them. People who came in hordes, and committed various acts of nastiness and folly, from clogging up roads and dropping litter to taking out small boats and needing rescue – to be grockle-grappled, as the coastguards put it. Not that he was really anything but a grockle himself. But he liked to think that his input had been benign. Apart from the dramatic rescue of Tucker's Hay, he'd resuscitated the equally dilapidated cottage in the village for Terry and Marie. What food he didn't grow he bought locally; he had the Range Rover serviced in Newton Abbot; he did everything he could to get himself assimilated into the community. One of these days, he reflected, as he looked across the landscape, he might even find himself on his knees in one of those squat grey churches. That should complete his de-grocklisation.

Meanwhile the cars continued to pour in, making for beauty spots they could drop into as if they were local parks or garden centres. When the summer came, Terry had said, he'd have to do something to ensure his privacy, back at Tucker's Hay. Build up the front wall, something like that. Put up notices to deter trespassers. Conrad hadn't made up his mind yet. Oh, Terry had made sure he'd got planning permission for the wall, but walls had two effects. They might stop visitors looking – and getting – in. But they'd also stop him looking out. And it had been the view from the front of the house that had sold it to him in the first place.

Ah, the car park was beginning to fill. Time he took himself home. He strode down the long grassed slope, knowing that by the end of the season it would be pitted and scoured by the thousands of feet that had trodden it. Yes, his included. Though maybe he should take up Elspeth's offer to spend the summer in the South of France. He grimaced: that would imply commitment, wouldn't it? And he didn't want to mislead her. And there were plenty of other places he could retreat to, if only Terry and Marie could leave the village. But he couldn't even ask them, not with Marie's mother failing and Marie herself pregnant.

Well, as his dad would say, things had a way of working themselves out. He'd just have to wait and see.

A bunch of horses was crowding into the car park. Some stupid sod had no doubt produced food, forgetting that the animals would be hungry after the long winter up on the moors. And that horses could be big, aggressive creatures, with teeth to bite and hooves to kick, for all they looked like refugees from Thelwell.

'Just get in the car and shut the door gently,' Beth said, as calmly as she could. But Emma was so slow she now had a car half-full of horse. 'And I'll back out very slowly and drive out. Then they'll go away, and we can come back. OK?'

'But it's got its head in!'

'I can see that. But start shutting the door so it can feel it pressing on its neck and I'll start the car and that'll make it move.'

'But what if it doesn't?' Emma was well on the way to hysteria.

'Just do it.' Beth's voice was calm but icy.

'He's going to bite! I know he's going to bite me!'

'Punch it on the nose then. And do as I say!' Beth put the car into gear and revved. The horse stayed put. OK. See how it liked having its neck nudged by the moving car.

It didn't. For a moment it shuffled sideways, but at last,

as Emma finally got it into her head to do the obvious, it withdrew. Beth kept the car moving, slowly, purposefully. The herd stood its ground. Then – prompted by someone yelling and waving his arms – it scattered. Smiling and waving a grateful hand, she pulled on to the road. Surely that was – no, it couldn't have been.

'Right,' she said brightly, 'a quick drive round what passes for the block out here, just so that the ponies forget us, and then we can come back. OK? Oh, come on, Emma, it isn't the end of the world! Or we can go on to Watersmeet if you'd rather. How about that?'

'I just want to go home,' came the wail from her passenger.

Beth bit her lip. So much for the breath of pure air she'd been longing for all week. Why on earth had the stupid girl produced an apple anyway? Beth had been quite explicit: these were wild horses, not the tame pets of her school friends. It was wrong to feed them. It made them aggressive. It encouraged them to stray on to the road in pursuit of other food-bearing cars, which caused accidents to themselves and humans. 'Don't even think about feeding them,' she'd said. So Emma had got out of the car the moment she'd parked and waved a nice juicy apple – God knew where she'd found it – at a dozen tough ponies. They'd jostled each other, they'd jostled the girl, they'd jostled the car. They'd taken no notice of Emma's whimpers or of Beth's yells. It was only when Beth had come up with the car idea that things had started to get better. And then that man had finished her good work.

Damn it all, she'd have her breather anyway. She'd earned it, and Emma had earned a lesson. She swung the car off on to a wide verge.

'What are you doing?' Emma asked.

'I'm parking here for a second. The sun's coming out, and a short walk won't hurt us, surely. Up as far as Hay Tor.'

Emma slumped further into her seat. 'It's miles and I'm cold and I need a ladies'.'

*   *   *

They were driving along some river or other – not that you could see much, but Beth said it was the scenic route – when Emma had her bright idea.

'I suppose I couldn't drive for a bit?' she asked. 'Only it's a nice quiet road, and I ought to keep in practice.'

'You passed your test then? Oh, well done.'

But Beth made no attempt to pull over.

'So can I?'

Why didn't Beth answer? Was she preparing a bollocking about the damned horses? She'd been ever so quiet ever since lunch. No, ever since the horses. She'd been quite chatty over lunch. They'd found a pub with a pool table, and Beth had shown her how to play. She'd even paid for her to play with a couple of lads who'd challenged her. And laughed at her when she tried to play darts.

So why had she got all ratty about the horses? Anyone could see they were hungry, poor things, and the least Emma could do was to give them the apple she'd saved from the cheeseboard. It hadn't been very nice having the horse put its head through the door, but then that man had turned up and saved them.

'I mean, I've got flat shoes and everything,' Emma prompted, virtuously.

'I know.' She didn't sound very convinced. 'But I'm afraid my insurance won't cover you. So it can't be today. Not until I've made a couple of phone calls. I'm sure it won't be a problem.'

'But I feel well enough today. And Dad always lets me.'

'Emma – I told you. The car's only insured for me to drive. No one else. So you'll just have to wait till I've had the policy amended.'

Emma subsided. She recognised that note in Beth's voice. It meant you couldn't push her any more. Where were they now? Shaldon. Another more-dead-than-alive place. God, why had she ever come down here?

*   *   *

39

Beth retired to her study. The following day there was a briefing session for head teachers up in Bristol and she'd been asked to do a presentation. She'd prepared all the overhead projector slides and hand-outs already, thank heaven, but there was still work to be done. She'd better get on and do it. It was, after all, what heads did on Sundays. Usually she could work in peace. Now she had to shut out the noise surging up from the television. Goodness knew what the girl was watching: whatever it was came with gales of canned laughter.

It was all very well telling herself that an assertive woman would go and tell her to turn it down. She had a feeling that Emma would see any request as yet another criticism or denial of her rights. Which, of course, it was. From Emma's point of view.

Hell! this was Beth's fault, of course. She should have known better than accept a teenager into her home – in term time, at least. She had set no parameters, established no rights or responsibilities. She didn't have a contact number for Sylvia and Russell, wherever they might be. She didn't even know when they might be back. Stupid, stupid woman, she castigated herself. She should have known better – she should have done better.

Meanwhile, she'd better finish this – thank goodness she'd have time on the train for a last-minute check tomorrow morning – and dig out her insurance details.

'It's not fair! Why can't I?' Emma took the policy document Beth had dug out but didn't lower her eyes from the television.'

'It's part of my policy: there.'

'But why twenty-five? I'm old enough to vote and everything.'

Beth tried not to sound headmistressy. 'It's a matter of risk. I suppose what the insurance company is trying to do is prevent loads of inexperienced teenage lads trying to drive sports cars like mine.'

'I'm not a lad. I'm a girl.'

Beth managed not to snort. She – and Christopher – had had ample evidence of that, hadn't they? 'I'm afraid they regard young drivers of whatever gender as too much risk. And it's only by excluding them that they manage to bring premiums down to a rate I can afford.' Which, goodness knew, was high enough.

'Couldn't you phone up or something? Get it changed? Dad did.'

Why waste breath arguing, when she knew what the answer must be? 'All right. I'll phone tomorrow, if I get a chance. But don't bank on it, Emma. And don't bank on my being able to afford it.'

She must have touched some nerve. Emma turned, raising an eyebrow exactly as she did. 'After all the money the government's pumped into education! Dad's shown me the pay scales!' She returned her attention to the television, using the zapper to turn the sound up and the conversation off.

Beth stared. Emma's rudeness was bad enough. But what chiefly interested her was where she'd come by the information. She had an unlovely vision of her family huddled together working out how much extra money her promotion had brought. Bastards! Resisting an urge to send Emma to her room and lock her in it, Beth managed to say quietly, 'Don't bank on that insurance, Emma. And if that's your attitude, don't even bank on my picking up the phone.'

Six

Funky or flowery? Beth had spent so long in the Bristol Marks and Spencer agonising over the choice of a dressing gown for Emma – she'd at last plumped for a peach satin one – that she'd missed the train she'd wanted, and had had to hang around forty minutes for the next, which drew in a further ten minutes late. She managed to find a seat, only to discover that the man opposite her glued himself to his mobile phone and yelled down it almost interminably. However short her own call had been – to warn Emma, or rather, the answerphone, that she was going to be even later than she'd said in her note, but that she'd bring in something from a chippie – she felt it had opened the floodgates and that she could hardly complain. She felt like doing more than complain when the connection at Exeter chugged out just as they arrived. When at last the next local train arrived, she managed to get a window seat. Even in the dusk she'd see waterbirds – maybe a heron or two – in the estuary and the Warren nature reserve. But storm clouds had brought night down early. At last she couldn't even see the sea. But she knew it was rough: it was smashing in plumes of spray over the windows as the train picked its way along the sea wall.

Desperate times called for desperate measures: she crammed on an ancient hat that might once have been waterproof. Almost blown off the tiny station, she turned inland, into the town.

The queue in the first chip shop was long enough to trail into the driving rain bouncing on the wet pavement.

Hang it all, she'd phone for a take-away pizza: at least that would give Emma some choice in the matter. Buffeted this way and that by the wind, and giving up on her umbrella, she headed for the path across the Lawn. Water lapping at her shoes? It wasn't often the Brook flooded! Retracing her steps hurriedly, she took to the pavement on the far side of the road running parallel to the Brook: that was still safe, though some shopkeepers had sand-bagged their doors. At this point her hat flew off, bowling purposefully towards the hatchery, where broods of orphaned ducklings were reared under warm lights. A year ago, Emma had delighted in them: now she was far too sophisticated for Beth to risk mentioning them.

She caught the hat and stuffed it into her pocket. She was so wet she might as well give in. She could always have a shower while they were waiting for the pizza.

Head down, eyes strained for the worst puddles, the overflowing gutters, she pushed on up the hill.

Emma gasped. God, what a mess Beth looked. By the time she came into the living room, she'd taken her coat and shoes off, and was towelling her hair, which was wet enough for trails to be trickling down her face. At least her mascara must be waterproof. But for some reason her feet were dark blue, and she was leaving blue footprints on the carpet. As for her shirt, she might have been in for some naff wet T-shirt contest.

Conrad rose to his feet. What on earth would he think of her aunt?

Emma looked up at him, under her lashes, to see if he was sniggering. He wasn't, but he flashed a smile down at her.

Beth stopped dead, but then wound the towel round her head, pushing the ends away. She managed a smile, but then spoilt everything by going all headmistressy and shoving a hand out.

'Beth Holyoake,' she said.

'Auntie – this is Conrad,' Emma said. 'He rescued me.'

She had an idea that Beth was about to laugh, but couldn't work out why. Conrad shook hands.

Before he could speak, Beth dived in. 'From what did you need rescuing?'

Emma looked up at Conrad. He looked back at her, but then turned to Beth again. 'She was in a bit . . . of a tight spot. So I helped as much as I could. Look, you're spoiling your carpet. Have you got a cloth somewhere? I could have a go at it if you liked.'

Beth looked down, opened her mouth as if to say something, then held up her hands like someone surrendering. 'Thanks. And Emma,' she had the cheek to add, 'why don't you make us all some tea or coffee while I get dry?'

'You look as if you've been swimming,' Emma couldn't help saying.

Conrad grinned. 'It's a naughty night to swim in,' he said in a funny voice.

Beth grinned back. 'Plenty of hurricanoes blowing out there,' she said. Well, if she was in a good mood, so much the better.

Beth had never had a quicker shower – it was one way of getting the shoe dye off her feet – or dried her hair more briskly. She'd no idea what Emma had been up to, but as sure as God had made little apples it was no good. And it was clear that her intentions as far as Conrad was concerned were far from honourable. Not that she could blame her – he was a very attractive man. Of course he was way too old for Emma, but what man would be able to resist a beautiful young woman appealing to his deep chivalric instincts – if chivalric was all they were.

There: her feet were pink again. Clothes? Yes, jeans and that cashmere sweater. And there was time to dab on some more make-up. She could hear them laughing. Yes, she had time. He didn't sound as if he was in any hurry to go anywhere. And she certainly was in no mood to drive him away. The funny thing was, she would have bet her summer holiday that Emma had no idea who he was.

He was still on his knees with a wad of kitchen towel when she reappeared. Emma had made black coffee: she must have finished the milk and not bothered to replace it. Thank goodness for the little pots of milk she always kept in the freezer for just such a moment. There'd be enough for their coffee, but Emma would have to turn out and get some for her breakfast tomorrow. And while Beth was microwaving the milk, she might as well defrost some biscuits – home-made, but not by her. No, they'd come from the Christmas fair. Along with the fine selection of chutneys, jams and pickles that lined her cupboard shelves.

Putting the milk and biscuits on the tray by the coffee, she sat down. Conrad dropped the paper in the waste bin and sat down too, but Emma withdrew behind the sofa and switched on her little-girl face. No doubt the little-girl voice would follow. And she'd be *Auntie*, which she hadn't been for years. What was Emma's game? To make herself look younger and more helpless, or to make Beth older and *ipso facto* fiercer and nastier?

'OK, Emma; confession is good for the soul. Why did you need to be rescued?'

She'd been right about the voice. 'Well, you see, Auntie, I had to go out. And it was raining so much I had to take the car. And I sort of got stuck in the car park.'

Oh, God. Driving without insurance. What had she done?

'How stuck and in what?'

Emma flushed, and looked desperately at Conrad.

'Under my car, Ms Holyoake.'

'Beth, please. Under your car. How much damage did she do to it?'

He gave an embarrassed shrug. 'Not as much as she did to yours, I'm afraid.'

Emma sobbed, 'It was raining and the windows were all steamed up and I never was any good at reversing.'

Beth gripped her hands till the knuckles hurt. There were a lot of questions to be asked, but she picked one at random. 'Where are the cars now?'

Conrad again: 'Mine's outside. Yours is – well, I got a friend to take it to his garage in Newton Abbott.'

She made her lips work. 'You realise that Emma isn't insured?'

Emma wailed, 'But you promised you'd phone.'

'Curiously enough, I did.' She'd sneaked out during lunch. 'Well then.'

'Well, it would have cost over two thousand pounds to insure a driver of your age to drive a car like mine. Provided,' Beth continued, fighting back a dreadful thought, 'he or she had a full licence. Do you have a full licence, Emma?'

She shook her head, her lip quivering. 'Not quite.'

No point in railing at her, for her half-truth yesterday. 'In that case my company wouldn't have insured you. The only company prepared to would have charged well over three thousand pounds, with a four hundred excess.'

'So you didn't pay?'

Beth turned to Conrad, keeping her voice as steady as she could. 'Do I gather it would have been cheaper to have done so?'

'Not quite. Look, forget about mine. It was designed to take a bit of punishment.'

'It sounds as if it took a lot, and I'm sure my brother would prefer me to pay.'

'It's going to cost an arm and a leg just to put yours right,' he said. 'A nice new one, too. Still,' he said, reaching up to clasp Emma's hand for a moment, 'I always wanted to be a knight in shining armour. And now if it's all the same to you, I'll take her out and feed her. Go and find your coat, Emma – and your wellies.'

She stopped halfway through the door. 'I haven't got any wellies.'

'I'll just have to carry you, then!' He looked across at Beth. 'Just forget about my car – OK?'

'We're not doing some . . . some deal . . . here, are we?' Beth forced the words out.

'I'll bring her back at whatever time you say,' he said. 'And that goes for whenever I take her out.' He surprised her with a smile. 'But you were right to ask.'

Beth stretched. Ten-thirty. She might just go down and fix herself a nightcap. She'd managed to get some work done. Not a lot. But enough to give the impression that she had tomorrow under control. But she'd kept thinking about her car. OK, her insurance provided her with a hire care. She'd just have to imply the damage was the other party's fault and it would be settled without recourse to official channels. And she could afford the repair – as Emma had pointed out, heads' salaries were generous enough. But that wasn't the point. Emma had not only broken the law and damaged two people's valuable property, she was now being rewarded for it. How else could you describe having a meal with Conrad Tate? However hard she tried to put policy documents and reports between her eyes and his image, it always came back. He was at least as tall as she, and try as she might to attribute his excellent figure to his expensive clothes, she couldn't convince herself. And you couldn't buy a face like that. Especially not eyes like that, a darker blue even than her own, striking in combination with hair which might or might not have been naturally blonde. It didn't matter, did it? With skin that looked weathered rather than tanned . . . He was too old for Emma, of course – but not old. Forty at most.

So what must she do about Emma? She'd have to persuade the girl to tell her parents, who could punish her as they felt fit. Or not. Meanwhile, she'd have to exercise maximum forbearance for a bit: she was so angry that with the slightest provocation she could hit her.

Right. Whisky or good old-fashioned cocoa? Hell! Not enough milk, of course! Nor any mugs. Guess what, Emma had stuffed the last one into the dishwasher and forgotten to set it going. Still, nice clean china for tomorrow, even if it meant getting up ten minutes earlier to empty it and put everything away.

It wouldn't take much to make her cry.

But she'd better not start, because that was Emma and Conrad arriving now. They seemed to be lingering in the hall. She was trapped, in her own kitchen. But then there was a tap on the door. Conrad put his head round it.

'Feeling any better?' he asked, smiling kindly.

'I'm fine; why d'you ask?' She wished she didn't sound so abrupt.

'Because when I told you about the car, you went green. It'll be all right, you know. Gordon's a good bloke – you'll never be able to tell. Did you eat?'

She clapped a hand to her face. 'I knew there was something I'd forgotten. And I was just about to have a stiff whisky.'

'Not good, on an empty stomach,' he said. 'Good job I brought this then.' He stepped inside, flourishing a plastic carrier bag. 'Seems to have leaked a bit. Have you got any newspaper? You don't want this staining your work surface.'

She reached some from the utility room without speaking.

'You know how you always order too much,' he said, unpacking foil boxes. 'Well, I've got this thing about wasting food. So I thought if you didn't fancy it I could always feed it to Falstaff. My pig. Where are your plates?'

She passed him one, at last managing a smile. 'I usually feed my spare naan to the ducks. Lager?' She took a couple of bottles from the fridge, and reached for glasses and bottle-opener.

'Thanks,' he said, pouring for them both. 'I stuck to water with the meal. Thought . . . it would be better. Oh, and I picked up some milk from a garage. It's in the hall. At least you'll be OK for breakfast now.'

She smiled. 'That's . . . very kind.'

It was only when he'd put the first plateful of curry into the microwave that she asked, 'Where's Emma?'

'I sent her to bed. She was knackered. She really was

very upset, you know. And glandular fever on top.'

Beth nodded, as he fished the plate out and popped naan in. 'She's always been such a sensible girl.'

'She blotted her copybook good and proper today, though. What are you going to do? Give me another plate and I'll warm this too.'

'Here.' She sat down, but waited till he'd finished before she said anything. 'I wish I could wave a magic wand so it had never happened. But what she did was wrong. It might have been some poor old biddy's car she bumped – there are enough of them round here, for goodness' sake.' Swallowing, she asked a question she'd so far put off. 'Where exactly did . . . the accident . . . take place?'

He looked at her from under his eyebrows, sitting down opposite her. 'You don't want to know.' He drank, and replaced his glass carefully.

'I'm afraid I do.'

'Okehampton.'

'What? What on earth was she doing out there?'

'Just wanted a drive. Come on, Beth, she's a kid. Kids do wild things. Didn't you?'

'Not quite as bad as that. But you did, didn't you?' She looked him in the eye. 'According to the media, you were a really wild lad, weren't you?'

He smiled without rancour. 'Not until I was a bit older than Emma.' He held her gaze. 'You won't tell on me, will you, Beth?'

Seven

The night was too foul for Conrad to do anything except concentrate on the road ahead. The main roads were awash. But the lanes up to Tucker's Hay were young watercourses, branches tangling down under the pressure of wind and water. Instead of garaging the Range Rover, he left it where it stood, as near the front door as he could get it. It was only years of his father's training that made him lock it.

And at last he was safe in the quiet and warmth of Tucker's Hay. The silence unsettled him after the noise outside. Scared him, even. No wonder Lear had enjoyed raging in the storm. It had kept his mind, too, off other, more personal matters. The sort that bugged you when you were cleaning your teeth. He watched the toothbrush distort area by area of his cheeks. So what the hell did he think he was doing?

He knew what he was doing, didn't he? He was falling for a pretty young face. How many times had he done it before? No, he didn't want to think about that now, any more than he had the other day out on the moor. But this time it would be different. This time he'd remember that she was young, that she was vulnerable – for God's sake, the poor kid had glandular fever! – and that she was no angel, but a human being capable of making mistakes. Quite big mistakes. Jesus, that poor woman's car.

Softly, softly. That was what Dad would advise. His agent's advice would be much more to the point. Don't fuck if you can't face the press. Hell, there'd been enough kiss-and-tell stories about him to last a lifetime. More than enough. It was bad enough a relationship ending, without the woman spilling everything to the *Sun* or whatever. News? Public interest? He thought not. No, the whole thing was bloody crazy.

And it was something he had to protect Emma from, wasn't it?

Poor kid. The sight of her face when she'd reversed that MG hard and fast straight under his wheel arch. Those huge brown eyes welling with tears, her mouth quivering. 'It's not even my car. It's my auntie's. Oh, what on earth do I do?'

The sensible thing would have been simply to exchange addresses. But the MG didn't look drivable. And it turned out her parents were out of the country and she'd no idea how to get back to Dawlish and didn't know which garage her auntie used. As for telling her auntie . . .

Well, a quick call on the mobile had brought Gordon out. No problem there. He'd hitched the lame car on to his wagon – no question of simply towing it while Emma steered. She'd wept again at the very suggestion. And it had occurred to Conrad that, much as he wanted to rescue her, putting her in charge of the Range Rover while he steered the MG wouldn't be the most sensible move in the world. Even though he'd thought at that point that she had a licence.

No wonder she'd been scared to tell Beth, who hadn't seemed to him at all like an auntie. In Emma's place he'd have been quaking. But Beth had taken it remarkably well, all things considered. God, what if she was one of those women who saved up their anger? What if she'd been calm and peaceful in front of him, only to let rip when she had Emma on her own?

He sat down on the edge of the bed. A gust of wind – less rain, now, perhaps – buffeted the window. Hell, what about Falstaff? How would he cope with the storm? Had Terry remembered to feed him? There was that curry Beth had said she couldn't manage. She'd seemed quite taken with the idea that Falstaff would finish it off.

No, there was nothing for it but to go and see. At least this time when he was out in the weather he could wear the oilskins and wellies Terry had told him to buy.

There was no sign of Falstaff, of course. Now he came to look at the sty, Conrad could see there was no need to worry. The sty was protected by the house from the worst of the weather – obvious you'd want pigs to the lea of you! Then the eaves of the sty roof were deep enough to protect the sleeping quarters. Yes, Falstaff should be all right in there. Great subterranean snores told him Falstaff *was* all right. Well, of course he was.

On the merest off-chance, though, he whistled.

'What the hell do you want at this time of night?' Falstaff demanded, almost as clearly as if he could speak.

'Got a treat for you. OK, it's a bit second hand. But I thought you might fancy it. How you doing, anyway?'

Falstaff sniffed, but sank on to his hindquarters for a scratch. Conrad tipped the scraps from the foil trays into the trough. Falstaff sniffed again.

'I want your advice, see. Do you think I should be back in Dawlish in time for breakfast? So I can protect Emma?' But then he recalled that one of her problems was that she didn't see anyone down here. Beth was out of the house before Emma was awake, and often didn't get back till after she was asleep. So why had the wretched woman insisted on having Emma to stay with her to convalesce? 'The poor child should be in Italy with her parents, shouldn't she? Flowery Tuscany – isn't that what D. H. Lawrence called it? – would have been a better place to recuperate than Devon. I mean, look at this!' Conrad spread his arms to confront the weather. 'Do you think that her aunt simply wants power? That must be it. Being in charge of a big school must give you a taste for bossing round young people. But it's odd her own brother can't stand up to her. He should have insisted on taking Emma abroad.'

Falstaff's eyes twinkled. 'It's a good job the father didn't insist: otherwise you'd never have met this whoever-it-is.'

Conrad snorted. 'God, it's bad enough talking to you, let alone pretending you're talking back. OK, old mate, see you in the morning.'

But sleep still did not come. Should he read a little? Press on with that enormously long biography of Virginia Woolf? No, it was late enough. He switched off the light again.

The funny thing was, Beth hadn't struck him as power-mad. Not at all. She'd struck him as a decent woman, maybe even vulnerable herself. When she'd heard about her car, she'd gone so pale he was afraid she might faint. And she hadn't screamed and raged when she'd learned that Emma hadn't even passed her test. He would have done, in her place. She wasn't vain, he'd say that much for her: although she'd arrived looking like a drowned rat, she'd been remarkably calm and dignified. But that might have cost her some effort: she'd looked totally washed out when he'd brought the spare food back. And he rather thought she might have been crying.

Thank God, she'd kept quiet about who he was. Now he thought about it, she must have recognised him straight away. There'd been that smile, quickly suppressed. But she'd had the grace to say nothing. And she'd readily agreed to keep his secret, as if she'd known he wanted Emma to value him as a human being, not an ageing pop musician.

Try as he might, he couldn't fit together all the details of the darling girl's face. There were the big brown eyes awash with tears. Yes. The lovely straight nose. That delicate mouth. The long fair hair framing the oval of her face. But he didn't have a sense of her face as a whole. Tomorrow he'd shoot off a whole film of her. And have it developed as quickly as possible. Yes . . .

Emma was the first thing he thought of as he woke up. But even as he rubbed the sleep from his eyes, he thought about that weird dream he'd had. He'd been trying to get the Range Rover across the old clapper bridge, and it had tipped over, into the fast-flowing stream. Well, he could account for that bit – the drive last night had been scary enough, and even now the sound dominating all others in Tucker's Hay was the swirl of rain in the gutters and drains. But why should the person fishing him out be not Emma, but Beth, complete with sou'wester and waders? When he saw her, he'd have to ask her if she owned such unprepossessing garments.

How on earth James Naughtie and John Humphrys did it Beth had no idea. But there they were, parrying repartee and sounding as if they were enjoying it, at – at WHAT hour of the morning? Why had she—?

And then she remembered why she'd had to set the radio alarm so early. Empty dishwasher. Get train. And, she realised, as she peered out of the window, pack spare clothes and shoes. She'd be soaked through by the time she got to Dawlish Station, and soaked again when she'd walked from the station to the bus and from the bus to the school. OK. Waterproof rucksack. Waterproof cagoule and trousers. Wellies. Well, if she expected the kids to turn up on bikes in this weather, perhaps it was best to show a bit of solidarity.

As for the dishwasher, that would have to wait till she got home – unless Emma had the nous to tackle it. To be honest, she couldn't even trust Emma not to shove her dirty breakfast things alongside the clean stuff. She'd better write a note reminding her to empty it first. Or would that be to infantilise her?

Infantilise her? She still wanted to marmelise her! But, as she closed the front door quietly behind her and headed into the morning, Beth had a very good idea that she wouldn't be seeing Emma alone for some time. The girl would hide behind Conrad as long as she could, wouldn't she? In her shoes, Beth would. Except that Beth couldn't even imagine doing anything as stupid, as – let's face it – as illegal as Emma had done. Somehow, sometime, the girl would have to acknowledge how wrong she'd been. But just at the moment the how and the when eluded Beth – and she suspected she wouldn't have a chance to worry about them until she got back home. A Monday off school always guaranteed a toppling Tuesday in-tray.

'Do you want the good news or the bad news?' Jane greeted her as she squelched her way into the office.

Beth pushed back her cagoule hood. 'Good.'

'The window-cleaners came yesterday.'

'Excellent. So what's the bad?' She pulled off her wellies, stripped off her outer layer, and held the cagoule, then the trousers, over the waste bin. They dripped irregularly.

'They broke your office window. They've repaired it, but it's a bit of a mess in there. I had to get off on time: Jeff was supposed to make sure they cleared up properly. I'll give him *properly* when I see him.'

Beth grinned. 'I'm sure you will. Anything else?'

'Another fire alarm broken. Down by the gym, this time. The fire people aren't best pleased.'

'I'm sure they're not. I'm not, either. I've an idea we have to pay for malicious call-outs, don't we? I'll have to make sure form tutors and year tutors put the fear of God into everyone. And . . . ?'

'And Mr Starling wants to see you. Again. Doesn't he have a day job? Ten, he suggested.'

She kept her voice formal, almost as if he could hear. 'Fine – so long as I've got a slot in the diary.' She still hadn't decided how she wanted this to go, had she?

'You have till ten thirty. Then you've got a meeting with the regional teachers' union rep.'

'Which union – hard or soft?'

'Hard.'

Beth grinned. 'Best coffee for her then: she's the one I was at uni with! Any idea what it's about?'

Jane frowned. 'I fancy it must be something serious. Her secretary wouldn't tell me.'

'We'll just have to see what good coffee will do, won't we? Oh – and Jane, get Jeff to turn the heating right

up. We can't have half the school dead with pneumo-
nia!'

'Clause Twenty-Eight,' Starling said, sitting down opposite
her, his frown lines deep. 'What do we do about it?'

'Exactly what the government tells us to do about it,
Christopher.' She spoke as calmly as she could, but knew
a crisis could be in the offing. 'Sex education has a very high
priority here, as I'm sure you know. Why do you ask?'

'Because I've had a complaint from a parent about a
member of staff.'

Oh, God. Oh, God. Beth braced herself. 'Which one? And
why did the complaint come to you, not me?' That sounded
officious, confrontational. 'After all, we have a proper procedure. Agreed by management, unions and governors.'

Christopher smiled. 'I'm afraid he thought a man-to-man
approach was best. So I promised I'd speak to you. Off the
record.'

Beth bit her lip. Anything off the record was a two-edged
sword. It might prevent a whole hideous raft of procedures
bringing publicity to all concerned. It might, on the other
hand, mean that an innocent party had no chance publicly
to defend him – or her – self against any allegations. 'Which
member of staff? In absolute confidence, of course.'

'Of course.' He shifted. 'It's . . . delicate. You see, he
hasn't been appointed yet. It's the new Art appointment.'

Beth looked at him steadily. 'The interview's next week.
I take it he's been short-listed?'

Starling nodded.

'What's the problem? What's this person alleging?'

'Beth – this is so awkward. He's suggesting that one of
the candidates may have a . . . a private life . . . that makes
him less than suitable. In his opinion.'

'You ask about Clause Twenty-Eight and you mention a
"him". Are we talking about a gay candidate?'

'I'm afraid so.'

'What if he's the best candidate for the job?'

'It was a very strong shortlist, I believe you said.'

Beth looked down at her hands, loosely clasped on the desk. No one would have guessed from them that her heart was pounding with anger. 'Very strong. All equally strong, apart from the sexual orientation of one of them. Is that what you're suggesting?'

'No, no. Not me. This parent. He suggested one wasn't quite as . . . as suitable . . . as the others.'

'Because he's gay. Simply because he's gay?'

'Elizabeth, I didn't say that.' He smiled, disarmingly. 'I'm simply passing on my contact's reservations.'

'Of course,' she said, returning the smile. She wanted to believe him. She wanted to believe he was decent and – yes, kind. 'How did he want us to act on these . . . reservations?'

'He's a great admirer of yours. I suspect he thought if you came out against this man – and I backed you – that would carry the panel.'

'I'm sure you told him you found the whole concept offensive – not to mention illegal?'

'Of course.'

Please let him be telling the truth!

'The problem is that he may make trouble later,' Starling continued. 'If and when this person were in situ.'

'Then it'll be our responsibility to support our colleague to the proverbial hilt, won't it? I'm so grateful you warned me about this, Christopher,' Beth said, leaning back to show how relaxed she was. 'I've been grateful for your support ever since I came into this post.' She looked at her watch. 'I wish I could offer you coffee – only I've got a union official coming in two minutes.'

'In that case perhaps we could use the two minutes to arrange something more than coffee. I hear there's a very charming restaurant out in Kenton – I wonder if we should see if it's as good as its reputation?'

She smiled, fishing out her personal diary. A meal. Why not? A quiet, intimate meal – to give her time to work out what she felt.

*　　　*　　　*

'Hmm,' Conrad said, kissing Emma's cheek, 'you smell nice.'

Emma flushed. 'It's some of Auntie's posh shower gel. She won't mind, OK – not when she knows it was to go out to lunch with you.'

'If you're sure lunch won't tire you out?'

'Positive. Where are we going? There's a good place in Taunton, Dad says.'

'Taunton it shall be,' he said, fishing out his mobile. 'What's the name of the place? I'll book us a table.'

'I don't know. Oh, I suppose we'll find it – Taunton isn't a very big place, is it?'

'Large enough to have more than one restaurant. Where's Beth's *Yellow Pages* – we'll read through that and see if any places ring bells for you.'

Emma wasn't quite sure about him calling her 'Beth'. 'Your aunt' would be better. 'Beth' sounded as if he was quite friendly with her. How long had they spent talking last night? It could have been till any time. Her glands had started to come up, so she'd taken aspirin and been asleep within minutes.

'I don't know where she keeps it.'

'Why don't you have a scout round? I mean, I don't want to go searching her house – I hardly know her.'

Cheered, Emma said, 'You could have a coffee if you liked – while I looked.'

'Great.'

At last she ran *Yellow Pages* to earth in Beth's office. Conrad was still in the kitchen.

'What on earth are you doing?'

He turned and smiled. He'd got great teeth. 'Just wondering where these plates live.'

'Why?' She put the directory down on the table.

'Because I thought I'd empty the dishwasher – save you a job. Here – didn't you see this note from Beth?'

'Oh, I thought I'd do it when I got in.' Or not. Beth wasn't

going to start ordering her around. Whose dishwasher was
it, anyway?

'But that means leaving your breakfast things and these
mugs – you know, I don't even know whether you take
sugar or not! – in the sink. And . . . well, it'd look nicer
if they were tidied away. And if I do it, it'll mean you can
keep your energy for something else.'

Emma bridled. He sounded horribly like Beth.

He put an arm round her shoulders while they looked at
the list of restaurants, but none of them sounded familiar.

'I don't know. Can't we just . . . go?'

''Course we can. I'll just check out the bathroom,' he said,
as if he was embarrassed.

She fetched her jacket – the short, pretty one – and stood
in front of the hall mirror, checking her lipgloss.

He had a funny expression when he came out. 'I think
we may have to put Taunton on a back-burner for a while,'
he said, 'and try a bigger place. You don't happen to know
where Beth buys her shower gel, do you?'

'No. Why? She's got plenty.'

'Not now she hasn't. I don't think the lid can fasten all that
well. It's . . . well, it's emptied itself all over the shower.'

'Oh, she won't mind. She'll have plenty of others.'

'I'm sure she has,' he said, his jaw getting quite stubborn,
so she'd better not argue any more. 'But I'm sure you'd
rather replace it, wouldn't you?'

Eight

B eth stepped off the little train – one carriage, that was all – into brilliant evening sunlight. Dawlish was at its newly washed best. The waterproofs now stowed into her rucksack, she looked ruefully down. She was a bit grown-up for striding through the town in wellies, wasn't she?

Tough. And in any case she didn't have to go through the town: she could walk right along the sea wall towards Teignmouth, cross the railway line at the footbridge, take her chance crossing the main road and pick her way through the lanes and paths round the back of the town. The bonus was that she could splash in as many puddles as she wanted. Which might, she realised as she set off, be quite a lot. All those on the breakwater, for a start.

Where the Brook met the sea the water boiled red with the sandstone washed down from the surrounding hills. Beyond that, however, was the open sea, the dazzling blue dotted with cargo vessels either sheltering in Lyme Bay or queuing to get into Teignmouth harbour on full tide. After the rain the air was brilliantly clear – she fancied she could just pick out Lyme Regis itself over to the east. However, she reminded herself grimly, this wasn't the moment for enjoying panoramic views. She should be heading home to confront whatever new domestic disaster might await her. As she set off along the sea wall, she wondered if she might phone Ken – not just to ask how he was getting on after his heart attack, but to chew over with him the day's events: Starling's hints, the union rep's anxieties about the latest government scheme, and yet another fire-alarm incident. Ken had been a wonderful mentor. Though he'd have been the likely choice for Head, he'd preferred not to apply, and when she'd got the job had been as fatherly to her as he was to the kids. Yes, given his subsequent illness, he'd been wise not to go for promotion.

'Beth! Beth? Penny for them!'

'Conrad!' Where had he sprung from? She stopped short, smiling. 'What are you doing down here?'

'Exploring. I thought Emma would be better for a bit of a zizz. And I wanted . . . you know . . . to check the place out.' He gestured at the railway line, the sea wall, the sea. 'I mean, these red cliffs – amazing.' He grinned at her.

'Have you come straight down that path? Because if you did, you've missed a little cove just round the corner – very pretty. And the bonus is that, though the path back is steep, it's not as bad as the one you came down.'

'Which would you normally take?'

She laughed. 'Depends on how fit I feel and how much I'm carrying. And on the weather and if I think I should dash back.'

'Given all those variables,' he said, frowning with mock seriousness and pulling his chin, 'what would your plan for this evening be?'

'The long way round via Coryton Cove. With the less steep path,' she added.

'And would my company mess up your walk?'

'Not at all.' She rather thought it would add to the pleasure.

'In that case, lead on, MacDuff. No,' he added, stopping short, 'it's *lay* on, isn't it? One of those things that folk are always getting wrong. Like "fresh fields", not "fresh woods".'

She laughed. 'Well, twitch your mantle blue, and walk this way.'

He didn't follow at once. He stood watching her, arms akimbo. 'I don't know if I can,' he said. 'You really need a posh suit and wellies to walk that way.' He demonstrated. 'Sort of tight-arsed and liberated rolled into one.'

This time her laugh was rueful: that summed her up exactly, didn't it?

'Not to mention carrying rather more than you should do. Let me take one of your burdens.'

She looked at him sharply. No, surely the remark was meant literally. 'I'm fine,' she said.

'My dad would smack my head if he saw me strolling along without a care in the world while you had that huge case and a rucksack. Come on, let me have them.' He stepped in front of her, holding out an authoritative hand. It was large, and well shaped, but the nails were short enough to suggest a lot of biting in the past. No sign of that now, though.

'It's rather heavy,' she warned, handing over the case. 'My homework for tonight.'

'Tonight? But it's after seven now.'

'Yes, I left early. I thought . . . well, having a visitor . . .' She suppressed all the words that might suggest she thought she should keep an eye on Emma. 'Mind the steps,' she added. 'They used to have a white strip painted on the edge to warn people, but it's wearing off. Sorry – next thing I shall be offering you a white stick and taking your arm!'

'Come on – give me the rucksack too.'

'That's just my wet-weather gear – hardly weighs a thing. And if your father would object to seeing a woman carrying her own stuff, imagine how my mother would feel if I let a man do it for me!' Actually, her mother wouldn't have turned a hair, being much more like Sylvia than like Beth. But sounding piously feminist wasn't on Beth's menu, not at the moment. 'Have you had a good day?'

'Hmm. Went to Plymouth.'

Plymouth? Why on earth? But it was none of her business. Not even if it wore Emma out? Except that he seemed even to have catered for that, sending her off for a rest.

They'd reached the short breakwater that protected Coryton

Cove. Beth usually stopped here, just to look and listen, before tackling the path up the side of the cliff. It seemed the view drew Conrad too. Dropping the case, he leaned forward on the railings. She leaned, too.

But not for long. She still had to eat, after all, and then sort out the paperwork on the Gifted and Talented Initiative.

He caught her sigh. '"What is this life . . ."' he began.

'The Department for Education and Employment don't encourage standing and staring,' she said.

'Is that teachers or pupils?'

'Forbidden for either, I'd have thought. If it's not part of the National Curriculum, we can't do it.'

'I'd have thought a GCSE in relaxation was long over-due,' he said. 'Given the amount of stress you teachers come in for.'

'That'd be about right: the teachers get the stress, the pupils get the qualification.' She took a reluctant last look at the beach and pushed away from the rail.

He followed suit. 'Why do you do it, then?' He held up her briefcase like the Chancellor on Budget Day. 'Unless you like weight-training, that is.'

She giggled. 'Funny thing is, I do. I used to, anyway. When I . . . when I had time,' she amended quickly. Days at the gym with Richard were long gone.

He shot her a look: was it because he'd sensed her hesitation or because he was checking for evidence of the weights? To throw him off whatever scent, she pointed back at the beach. 'I promised myself when I moved down here I'd run on sand every day – wonderful for stamina.'

'Didn't that Australian runner – Herb Elliott, was it? – do that?'

'Regularly. I managed it twice. But I've made some moves today to improve things. If I can get support form the governors and from the PTA. The trouble is getting girls interested in exercise – whenever they see sport on TV it's men, isn't it? So I thought we might introduce exercise machines – much 'cooler' than conventional PE lessons. We might even get them sponsored. And the bonus would be that the staff could use them after school.'

'So you're planning on getting home even later than this? Or are you going to move nearer the school?'

She turned to face him: 'Not bloody likely!'

'Ah,' he said grinning. 'That'd be Eliza Doolittle in *Pygmalion*, wouldn't it?'

Emma stretched, her mouth wide in a yawn. Hmm. She rolled on to her side, smiling invitingly, seductively. If only there were something more responsive beside her than her pillow. One day – one day soon – there would be. He'd be there, Conrad, naked, his face glistening with sweat, the dark hair of his chest rising and falling after their shared moment of passion. What would the rest of him look like? So far her experience of men had suggested that sex was more fun in films than in real life, but a man Conrad's age would do better, wouldn't he? He'd know how to give a girl a wonderful time. Oh, and she'd make sure she gave him one, too. Smoothing her hand over her hip, she posed like the nude in that famous picture – the woman with the black ribbon round her neck. Beth would know the name, of course, and the artist. Probably the year it was painted and what the artist liked for tea.

Where was he? It didn't sound as if he was watching TV or anything. What if she called him? He'd come in and see her like this and . . .

If only he wasn't so silly about this stupid glandular fever. As if a man of his age would get it. All this stuff about not kissing her on the mouth, in case she was still infectious. Anyone would think she'd got AIDS or something.

She sat up. Funny – the place was quiet as the grave. Maybe she'd better get up and see what was going on. She could even try out that dressing gown that Beth had bought. It looked pretty respectable, but you never knew – maybe it could be made more sexy. Even if it was just a matter of making sure the top gaped a bit and the tie emphasised her waist.

There – that wasn't bad. She posed in front of the dressing-table mirror. No, hitch it up one more inch or Beth would make some crack about catching cold. If she took both her slip and her bra off – there. And her pants, come to think of it.

The sound of voices outside made her look up. So who had Beth dragged home this time? Some sad bloke from school, toadying to her by carrying her bag! But it wasn't some sad bloke. It was Conrad. What the hell was Beth doing with her boyfriend?

'So there I was with this major hard-on, sitting in her aunt's kitchen drinking tea.'

Falstaff grunted sympathetically, though he made it quite clear that when it was as dark as this he preferred to be asleep.

'I'm in a bit of a cleft stick, aren't I? I can't – I really, really can't – risk getting glandular fever just before the US concert. And if glandular fever's the kissing disease, there's no way I want to get it by kissing even Emma. But there she is in this sleek dressing gown affair – peach satin – and if she leans forward I can see the shape of her breasts and . . . You can see her nipples pressing against the material. And then she crosses her legs. God Almighty. How did I keep my hands off her?' Even thinking about her made him clamp them to Falstaff's gate.

Falstaff grunted.

'Good job Beth was there. Oh, she noticed all right. Yes, both the dressing gown and my hard-on. There's very little, I'd say, that she misses. She gets this glint in her eye – rather like yours when you spot an apple, come to think of it – and you can see her trying not to smile.' Not always a straightforward smile of amusement, however. A lot of irony in Beth's smiles. 'She doesn't seem to have let on to Emma who I am,' he continued. 'It'll come out though, won't it? When I hop on that plane? She thinks I'm some sort of farmer, I think. Well, that's what I've been hinting at, of course. And it's not a lie. Funny, she's not asked to come and see the place.' Yes, that niggled him. He wanted to know all about her and her work – imagine, being stuck on the photograph-processing counter at Boots! – but she seemed quite disinterested in his. No, that was wrong. It should be *un*interested, shouldn't it? Did that mean she was uninterested in him?

Falstaff retired to his latrine corner.

Conrad decided it was time to retreat. There was, in any case, a thread of melody somewhere at the back his head. Maybe, maybe, he could . . . Yes!

At least the noise from the television – was Emma deaf? – ensured that Beth could make her phone calls in privacy. The first was the promised one to Ken Edwards, her deputy.

Although he asked after the school, Ken was really more concerned with his drugs and his diet. Who could blame him, after that big scare? Not Beth. But it was as if he'd left already. All she could do was ask what she hoped were intelligent and sympathetic questions about his exercise programme and reassure him that, though everyone missed him, he mustn't think about coming back before he was ready. In fact, though his sick note ran out at the end of the month, she'd bet it would be extended and extended. Soon he'd join the massed ranks of teachers who'd retired early because of stress: she'd bet her pension on it. Oh dear, she'd miss him.

Before she could make the next call, the phone rang. Jumping despite herself, she picked up the receiver.

'You don't sound very pleased to hear me,' Sylvia observed.

'Oh . . . oh, I was miles away.' With a bit of luck Sylvia wouldn't be. With a bit of luck Sylvia would be on English soil and heading purposefully in the direction of Devon with the express intention of removing her daughter.

'I have thought you'd be too busy to daydream,' Sylvia said.

There must have been a reply to that; but Beth couldn't think of it. 'How was your holiday?'

'Fine. In fact, we've had the most enormous piece of luck. We've met some people with a villa in Tuscany, and they've asked us to share it. So—'

'You'll be wanting Emma to come and join you?' Oh, thank all the holiday gods for that.

'No question of that, I'm afraid. It only sleeps four. In any case, she's quite settled with you, isn't she? After all, it'll only be a few more days.'

'So when will you be back?' Pin her down! You have to pin her down!

'Oh, we're not quite sure . . .'

'Sylvia, there are one or two probl—'

But the phone was dead. Damn and blast and a whole selection of more expressive expletives.

She slipped down to the living room. Emma was curled up on the sofa chewing her hair and flicking through a magazine Beth didn't recognise. Beth reached for the zapper and killed the sound.

'That was your mother on the phone . . .'

'Yeah – spoke to me earlier. Lucky cow. A week in Rome and now a fortnight in Tuscany.' Emma reached for the zapper.

'Hang on a bit. A fortnight!' A fortnight! A fortnight before she could have her house to herself again!

'Yeah.'

Beth took a deep breath. 'So where does that leave you?'

Emma stared. 'Here, I suppose.' She pressed the volume button. There were gusts of laughter and loud applause.

But not, Beth reflected, pouring a stiff whisky, for her own wimpish performance.

Nine

'I insist,' Christopher said, 'absolutely insist. After a day like this you're entitled to a brandy with your coffee. Even if the coffee is decaffeinated,' he added, with a charming smile.

Beth nodded. After all, she was going to have to take a cab home. She hadn't had time to sort out a hire car, and the last train to stop at Dawlish left Exeter before ten. They weren't even in the centre of Exeter, but in Topsham, the sleek village-turned-suburb where Christopher lived.

'Thank you,' she said, smiling back.

The waiter withdrew.

'It has been a bit difficult,' she admitted. 'What with the fire service and the police – who'd have thought all those false fire alarms would be followed by the real thing? Oh, I thought the police would never go. All those questions. Still, I suppose arson is a dreadful crime. Especially with all those young lives at risk.'

They'd agreed not to talk shop over the meal; he'd said he wanted to see the frown lines leave her face. He'd been much less formal this evening – he'd told her about his marriage, his wife's death and his difficulties with his grown-up daughters. She'd told him a little more about Richard than she usually allowed to escape: not the real reason for their break-up but about the hobbies they'd shared, and his resentment over her career. After months as merely professionals with a shared interest in the school, it seemed they might be becoming friends. And maybe more.

'Yes,' he said, running his eyes over her face as if

checking it. 'I think we can talk about the fire now.' He put his hand gently over hers. 'It was most unfortunate I couldn't come to the school when your secretary rang me to break the news. How much damage did it do?'

'Not much, but enough. Well, the stationery store's pretty central to the school, even if the damage was confined to that area. What paper wasn't burned was turned into papier mâché. As you know, the kids have loose-leaf folders rather than exercise books for most subjects. So that paper won't be hard to replace. But there's computer paper, all our headed paper – everything.'

He gave a serious smile. 'Beth – I hope you won't take this the wrong way. As you know, I try to keep my business interests and the school completely separate. But I do have some influence in a printing firm. Would you care for me to use it?'

'Aren't we required to ask for tenders from all our suppliers?'

'Part of that tender must include delivery time. How soon could your usual supplier deliver? I think I could promise you delivery of the bulk of your needs by . . . the day after tomorrow. The rest by Monday. And – just to make it a little more . . . official . . . shall we say – perhaps you could hint at your usual supplier's terms? So I could guarantee our tender would be favourable.'

He'd never asked anything like this before. It wasn't entirely moral, of course – maybe not legal, come to think of it. But a quick phone call this afternoon had come up with the depressing news that she couldn't expect more than a trickle of replacement supplies and that she'd be lucky to get lined A4 in time for the summer exams.

The touch on her hand became a light grip. 'I'm sorry. I've put you in an awkward position.'

She shook her head. 'You're rescuing me from an even more difficult one. It's just the business of the tenders I don't like. Though as Chair of the Governors you're entitled to see them, of course.'

'Which I've tried to avoid doing, to avoid any conflict of interests. You'll recall my leaving the room while such matters were discussed.'

Offhand, she couldn't. But the coffee and brandy were already in front of them.

'Why don't you simply leave the file on your desk tomorrow? I can glance at it while I wait for you to discuss the situation – more officially than we're doing now. And I promise I won't say what I want to say now: I've never seen you looking more delightful.' His grip shifted; he lifted her hand to his lips.

She couldn't doubt the invitation in his eyes. And much of her would have liked to accept it. But even as she speculated on the likely pleasures of sex with him, it occurred to her that her non-arrival at home – even her late arrival – would put a card into Emma's hand she didn't want her to have. No, a taxi it would have to be. And from the restaurant, not his home, wherever that was. Within walking distance, presumably: he wouldn't be attempting to drive after all the wine they'd had, surely. She allowed herself a glance at her watch, a little jump of surprise.

'Emma!' she said. 'Time I was getting back to her.'

'Surely that young lady is old enough to take care of herself,' he said.

Beth looked him full in the eyes. 'Do you think so? I'm terribly afraid she's all too aware of her effect on men, without realising the possible consequences. She's just acquired a wildly unsuitable boyfriend – her parents expect me to chaperone her.' They would if they knew, at least. Not that Conrad was at all unsuitable. He was just the sort of stabilising influence Emma might need. But twenty years was far too big a gap between a man and woman. Far too big. She suppressed a shudder.

'Beth, Beth.' He shook her hand slightly. 'I've told you: you work so hard and such long hours, you're entitled to be cosseted in your free time. You shouldn't have to be nannying someone else.'

She found herself turning her hand to return the pressure. 'That's very kind of you. And I promise you I shan't try to keep her a day longer than I have to.' There: an implicit promise. Now was the time to make her exit. But she found herself deferring to what she was sure he'd want. 'Christopher, I wonder if you'd ask the waiter to call me a cab.' As if she hadn't organised her own transport for years!

But he liked her little show of dependence. 'And when are we going to do this again?'

'Very soon: we were going to try that restaurant in Kenton, weren't we? Was it Tuesday, next week?'

'I've already booked a table,' he said. 'But there are a number of evenings between now and then. Might I hope . . . ? No, I'm sure I shall hear that wretched word again: *but*.'

'It's a very real but,' she said. 'Niece apart, you appointed me to run the school. And you warned me at interview that it would take over my life. And it has.'

'Any news of your deputy?' he asked sharply. 'It's time you had a replacement.'

'He's far from well.'

'Time we put together a premature-retirement package,' Christopher said briskly. 'We'll discuss it tomorrow.'

Falstaff clearly drew the line at Chinese food. But he snuffled at Conrad's pocket.

'Ah, you can smell the apple, can you, you old rogue? You know, I'm never going to be able to turn you into bacon. It's a good job you're pedigree – you'll be able to have some fine old times adding to the gene pool, won't you?'

Falstaff accepted the apple.

'Should be apples for teachers, shouldn't it? A whole crate of them for head teachers, I should think. Except that she wasn't there tonight. Out on the razzle, Emma said. So Emma and I could have bonked each other brainless if we'd wanted. Oh, I did. And she did. My God, she's one sexy

71

young woman. And knows it. But it isn't just the glandular fever business. She's *so* young, Falstaff. When we're out there are these great gaps when I can't think of anything to say. Well, not without blowing the gaffe. And I want her to love me for who I am, not what I am.'

Falstaff tried the beansprouts again, rejected them again, and tried another Chinese morsel.

'My God! Pork! No, don't eat it – it might be your grandfather in there!' Shit, that was how BSE spread, wasn't it? Feeding cows meat products? Except that cows were herbivores, and Falstaff was indisputably an omnivore. He'd tried telling Emma about Falstaff, and these midnight talks they had. No. He didn't think she'd become a Falstaff fan. Not if her only reaction was that pigs were filthy smelly things, and she hoped Conrad wouldn't expect her to go within miles of the sty.

Perhaps things would be better when they could sleep together. Not much longer. Only a week to go before he left for the USA, one week there and then – oh, yes.

'Break it to her? Yes, I suppose that'd be the term. She's not going to like it, is she? Especially if she thinks it's for some farmers' convention. So I will have to tell her, won't I? If only I could be sure she'll be . . . discreet.'

Falstaff snorted.

'Tell you what, mate, I shall be glad when my dad's back from Oz. I could do with a good natter to him. No, the phone's not the same, is it? And we always approach these things sort of sideways. I can't just phone him and say, "I've got this new girl and she's young enough to be my daughter." Christ! She is, isn't she? Emma's young enough to be my daughter.'

If only she could persuade Emma to pick up the bathmat and hang up her towels. And not, come to think of it, use Beth's towel. She grabbed the lot, and shoved them into the washing machine. No one would hear it chuntering to itself in the utility room. All she had to do was remember to empty the machine in the morning. Or leave a note for Emma to do it. Conrad, more likely. Who'd have expected a man with his lifestyle to be so domesticated? And considerate in other ways: she was damned sure it wasn't Emma's idea to hot-foot it to Plymouth to replace her shower gel. And the money wouldn't have come out of Emma's purse either. That was another thing she hadn't arranged with Sylvia and Russell: money. They'd assured her they'd given Emma enough cash for a week – but this week was now spreading into three, wasn't it? She'd never asked them to pay anything towards Emma's keep in previous holidays, but there was a vast difference between a weekend and the present situation. How much pocket money should she have, anyway?

And there was still the business of the car, of course.

She reached out fresh towels and laid them in a pile.

Emma wasn't too keen on general bathroom tidiness. At least it wasn't Beth's toothpaste she left drooling from the tube. But her clutter was beginning to feel invasive – the cleanser and toner. Beth always kept hers in her own room – she'd suggest Emma did the same. Where her contraceptive pills emphatically should live.

Oh, my God! Contraception! Fancy Emma being more streetwise than she was! If her life was going to include sex again, it was time for her to seek advice. Tomorrow's job. Along with organising a car and talking to Christopher about Ken.

Not to mention letting him see that tender.

No matter how many times she told herself she was only doing it for the good of the school, it was a long time before sleep arrived. And when it did, she dreamed about paper and huge, billowing fires.

Ten

'You wonder how he does it, don't you?' Jane asked, stuffing files into the middle drawer of one of the cabinets in her office. 'Runs all these businesses and still manages to spend half his life here.'

'Starling, you mean?' Beth asked, not as idly as she'd have liked. It was unlike Jane to step as far out of line as she had this last couple of mornings. And she liked Jane, and trusted her judgement. 'It's only these last few weeks he's really been around more than you'd expect.'

'Hmm.'

'That's a very meaningful *hmm*, if I might say so.' She leaned back, half-sitting on Jane's desk. 'Come on, Jane, spit it out.' After all, they'd had other off-the-record conversations.

'Who said there was anything to spit out?'

'You did. Come on; bring your coffee into my room, and give me every last bean.'

'You spill beans,' Jane objected. But she rammed the last file home, and closed the drawer with a shove of the knee. 'It's just that I heard,' she continued, busying herself with the kettle she kept beside her desk, 'that you're seeing each other these days. You know – socially.'

'He took me out last night to get the low-down on the fire,' Beth said. Yes, she'd sounded defensive.

'And the concert the other night?'

'My God! Are the CIA operating round here?' Beth tried to laugh.

'Just small-town jungle drums,' Jane said. 'My sister did

the catering for the Cathedral concert and she dropped into that place in Topsham because her brother's the chef.'

'So is there anything I should know about Starling?' Beth asked, woman to friendly woman. And wished she hadn't. The tenders! Well, the file was now tucked into the depths of her desk, until Jane had gone home and it could be slotted back into the system.

Jane made the coffee, picked up both mugs and looked at Beth's door. Oh, dear – what was Beth about to hear that she wouldn't like? She opened it, letting Jane through first.

Parking the mugs on Beth's desk, Jane sat on her usual dictation chair.

Beth took her mug and carried it to the window. 'Well?'

'Well, I've not really heard anything bad about him. Nothing at all. It's just . . . well, your predecessor. He did with her exactly what he did with you. Kept her at arm's length, and then started haunting the place, and then started taking her out. Doesn't mean anything, of course. Just means he likes headmistresses.'

Beth froze. Urged by the governors, her predecessor had sold all that land to pay for the new Language Block. Any particular governors? Any particular governor? When had she done it? And who owned the land now, with all those little houses on it?

She made herself relax. 'What else, apart from liking dominant women?'

'Ooh, is he into that? Do you have to tie him up, Beth?'

'Not yet! He seems a nice enough man. Quite shy, considering . . . you know, his position here.'

'He's certainly got a good name in the city. That firm of his, the one making the furniture – it gives a lot of men work they wouldn't have.'

Pity the furniture was so nasty.

'Any fingers in any other pies?' Beth asked.

'Well, he's big in the parish church in Topsham – he's given ever such a lot of money to restore it. And he helped fund that youth centre, down by the quay. It's just . . . it's just somewhere deep down, Beth, I don't like him. And there's no reason. I mean, he always asks after me and the kids. Listens to the answer, too, as if he's interested. No. No side to him.'

'But you don't like him.'

Jane drained her mug in one and sat staring at the dregs. 'No, it's funny, but I don't. Otherwise, I wouldn't have said anything. No, it's about time you found a decent man. You might even marry and settle down and have half a dozen kids. No, only joking! I've just got you run in nicely – I don't want a new boss, no thank you.'

'Well, your present one's still got a load to sort out. Look at this lot, Jane. It isn't as if you didn't filter half of it out for me. I seem to be getting slower and slower.'

Jane peered at her. 'It isn't your time of life, is it? You know, the Change?'

'God, I'm not forty yet! I know I feel eighty and might look ninety—'

'You know you don't. You've got a lovely figure and nice skin. But you do seem to be losing some oomph, if you take my meaning.'

Beth sat against the window sill. 'Tell you something: I miss the teaching. I really do. And I'm beginning to dread it when an education minister so much as opens his or her mouth.'

'Don't we all? Not just teachers, parents too, you know. And the kids, I dare say. Worrying about where to go after here.'

'And that's something else,' Beth admitted. 'I like older kids, too. I want to see them through to university, not decant them into college for their A levels or whatever. Perhaps it's time I started taking the *Times Ed*, Jane. While I'm still young enough to get another job, and you're still young enough to train someone else.'

They chatted so long that Beth insisted on calling a cab to get Jane back home. As for herself, she still had another couple of hours' work to do before she could leave. And she had to slide that file back into Jane's system. She felt soiled as she did it.

There was a fair chance, thank goodness, that Emma would be in bed and asleep by the time she finally got home, and indeed her curtains were drawn. She felt her shoulders relaxing. But there was a light on in the living room. Conrad.

He stood up, putting his fingers to his lips and pointing towards Emma's room.

'Stayed on because I was hoping to catch you,' he said, sitting down again, but folding the *Guardian* and pushing it to one side. 'My mate phoned with news of your car. The middle of next week, he reckons. Could be earlier but his best paint-sprayer's off for a couple of days.'

She dropped her briefcase. 'Any idea how much it'll cost me? Do I need to sit down?'

He looked at her as if he were the teacher. 'I told you: it's Emma's parents who need to sit down. I mean, she can't pay, not on the pittance she gets; but you shouldn't have to. Tell you what, I'll tell them what happened. When she takes me to meet them.'

She did sit. Quite suddenly, quite hard. The last thing she'd have expected was him to take such a disinterested line.

'I should think you'd have other things to worry about when you meet them. Which all sounds very old-fashioned and charming, by the way.'

He sat too. 'She thinks it's old-fashioned too. But in the pejorative sense. Funny,' he continued, leaning forward, 'I used to think that should be spelt with an "r" – like in "perjury". And "minuscule" with an "i" in the middle, as if it were "mini-something".'

'You're in the wrong job,' she laughed.

A shadow saddened his face. She felt too worn to ask the right questions.

'Have you eaten?' she asked, rather too brightly. 'Because I haven't. There's some wine in the fridge, too.'

He looked at his watch. 'You've been working till this time of night?'

She shook her head. 'The trains are badly timetabled, that's all. I just missed one and had to wait for ever.'

'But you should eat regularly. My dad had to give up work with his ulcer. Missed meals and stress – you have to pay for messing around with your body. Why don't I nip out for some food for you?'

She stood, shaking her head. 'I'll get a pizza from the freezer. And swig that wine while I wait.'

He followed her to the kitchen. When she'd shoved the pizza into the oven he said, 'Here, why don't you sit down and let me rub that neck for you? Before it sticks? You look like a bird hunting for something to peck!'

She sat down, slinging her jacket on the table – good job he'd wiped it after he and Emma had eaten their chips. He'd have hated her to get grease on it.

He dug in, his fingers and thumbs finding sore spots. 'Hey – I know you said you did weights – have you taken to carrying the world on your shoulders or something?'

'Why?'

For answer he pressed into the knots he'd been pussy-footing round.

'Jesus Christ!' she gasped.

He rubbed more gently. 'I didn't know you swore,' he said.

'Heads are human beings too,' she said. 'Cut us . . .'

'Do you not bleed?' he finished for her. '*Merchant of Venice* – right? Now, how about this bit here?' It was good, feeling the muscle relax. He could have done with tackling the whole of her back, but he could hardly suggest it. 'There,' he said at last. 'Have a glass of that wine, and then pop yourself into a nice hot bath. Aromatherapy oil, that sort of thing.'

'I don't know when I last had a soak,' she said. 'Brisk

morning shower, that's me.' She took the wine from the fridge, poured it into the glasses he'd reached for her. She sniffed. Then poured both away. 'Not worth drinking. Good job I always have a back-up.'

'Be more sensible if you got a better corkscrew – here, let me.' He held out his hand.

She shook her head. 'What if you spiked yourself on it? With that US concert only next week! Why no tour, by the way?'

'How did you know about that?'

'The paper.' She touched a finger to her lips. 'I haven't said anything. Not that you won't have to. Why no tour?'

'Because – oh, don't ask. Not at the moment.'

'There's something I have to ask. Are you taking her with you or leaving her here?'

He sat down heavily on the chair she'd left. 'She doesn't know what I do, so I can't take her. Still doesn't. She – her generation – I'm ancient history, *pre*history. That's why the Shea Stadium concert's my last. That's why no tour. Finito. Kaput. Oh, I'll still do albums – I'm working on one right now.'

'Are you?' She smiled as if it was the best news she'd had all week. 'Here – try this.'

It was good wine. Well, head teachers earned enough to buy good wine these days, according to his dad. Not like in his day, when teachers were paid a pittance. He looked around. The kitchen would have set her back a bit, and the bathroom was obviously newly fitted. The living room – good solid comfort there. But that was no reason why she should fork out for the car repair.

'How do you work everything out?' she asked. 'Do you work it out on the guitar and then transfer it to manuscript paper? Or have you got some gizmo to do everything for you these days?' She topped up his glass and sat down.

It was as easy as talking to Falstaff – all the stuff about having to think so hard about the technology that he couldn't grasp the music. She listened seriously.

'But when you get more confident, maybe you'll be able to work straight on to the computer,' she said. 'I know a writer who used to do everything longhand in pencil, and now he has to take a laptop everywhere. Ah, my pizza!'

She cut it into slices, pushing the plate to him. Before he knew it, he was outside a couple of slices, not to mention another glass of wine. He looked at his watch. Nearly twelve.

If he hung round till he was fit to drive, she'd be dead on her feet – and she had to get up early to catch a train. He bit his lip. Even he'd think it was a bit extravagant to take a cab out to Tucker's Hay – always assuming, of course, he could raise one at all at this time of night.

She looked at him, her head slightly on one side. 'If you want to help me finish the bottle, I've got a sofa bed in my study. There's only one problem: you'll be trapped there till morning once you go up – access is via my bedroom.' She grinned. 'But I'm up betimes. Just after six these days.'

'How loud's your alarm clock?' he asked, feigning terror.

'Oh, I could give you a morning call if it didn't wake you!'

She had the most beautiful legs, and didn't seem to know, the way she led him unselfconsciously up the staircase. And to what a room.

'Oh, Beth – I could live here,' he said. 'It's beautiful – all this wood. And all these books.'

He wandered round touching them while she found sheets and a duvet. Then, although she said she could manage, he helped her pull out the sofa bed and make it.

'You'll find a toothbrush and towel in the bathroom,' she said. 'And if you can manage with Bic razors, there are some in the cabinet. Give me a whistle when you've finished. I'll be in the living room.'

'You won't be trying to work, not at this time of night,' he said sharply.

'Only if I can't sleep. And I should think the wine will have fixed that.'

It was strange, hearing her move around quietly below him. Very soon, however, came a faint click as she switched off a light. Below the floor at that end of the study Emma would be asleep. He blew her a kiss. Then one to Beth, for her kindness.

It was too hot under the duvet. He wound back the blind from the window directly over his head and opened it slightly. When he switched off the lamp Beth had placed beside his bed, the stars seemed very close.

Eleven

It was best to let Conrad sleep on in the study. So Beth eschewed the radio – wouldn't he love the word? – even though it meant showering and dressing without Humphrys and Naughtie interrogating people on *Today*. She even left her shoes by the front door with her bag and briefcase. She was just embarking on a silent breakfast when the kitchen door opened.

'Any chance of a coffee?'

'Conrad!'

He was already shaved and presumably showered – his hair was damp, tending to curl.

'Or better still, some of that fruit juice. I thought I'd make an early start too. Back home.'

'You're not going to wait . . .' But it was a stupid question – obviously Conrad wasn't going to wait until Emma woke up – so she bit it off halfway through.

His grin was ambiguous. Was it sheepish or almost distressed? 'I . . . well, I've got work to do, Beth. And . . .'

Yes, he was anxious, wasn't he? He was biting his lip and making a gesture of helplessness. 'She's in there and I can't even kiss her!' he blurted.

'Oh, the kissing disease!' She stifled her laughter. 'But that only applies in the incubation period, surely.'

He turned from her so she couldn't see his face. 'Does it sound terrible to say I can't take the risk? The Shea Stadium concert – how many people would it let down? And the gig's going out across all the major networks. If only you'd got a satellite dish you might be able . . . if you wanted, that is . . .'

'Of course I'd want to. Conrad – if I talk another minute I shall miss that train.'

He turned back. 'Finish your breakfast. I'll run you in. And go back home from there.'

'Where's home?'

'Up on Dartmoor. Not far from Hay Tor.'

'King's Barton School's miles out of your way. And the traffic will be nicely snarled up.'

'Just finish your toast. OK?'

Beth didn't want to go into school, did she? As they picked up the main road for Exeter – Beth had guided him through back lanes to the A380 – Conrad told her the joke his father used to tell, rather too often, really:

Mummy, I don't want to go to school.

You've got to go to school, son.

But the kids frighten me and the teachers hate me. I don't want to go to school!

Well, son, you've still got to go in. You're the headmaster, after all . . .

He'd made her laugh, but if he thought her smiles were sometimes ironic, there was no doubt this was a self-mocking laugh.

'So why don't you do something else?' he asked.

Had he gone too far? She was silent so long he was afraid he'd upset her.

'Look,' he said, 'just tell me to mind my own business – I didn't mean to offend you.'

She turned to face him, smiling. 'Offend me? Oh, Conrad, of course not. It's a question I often ask myself, these days. The trouble is, I'm not sure what that something else is. You see – oh, this sounds, as Emma would say, pretty gross – but I'm very well paid and enjoy the things my salary brings. If I went back into teaching proper, I'd have to take a big cut. And that's what I'd really like to do – get back to working with kids. That's why people become teachers, after all. To be with kids.'

'But you've got a whole school full of kids.'

'Most of whom I never see. Oh, I deal with the very worst troublemakers, and occasionally get to pat the heads of high achievers. But I never get to see the ordinary pupils.'

'But you must be more than a figurehead, the hours you work.'

'I am. I'm like the captain of a big ship, I suppose. I've overall responsibility for everything, from the food the passengers eat for breakfast to the general avoidance of icebergs. But it's overall responsibility: not hands-on doing. I used to work in an inner-city comp in Sheffield. I mean, a tough school, with huge, huge problems. No one could survive teaching there more than a few years without being overwhelmed. But my stint there was one of the most satisfying I've ever had. I changed things. Maybe for only a very few kids. But I made a difference to them.'

'What about different ways of working with kids?'

'Such as?' She laughed. 'Oh, Conrad, I've been over this so many times in my head. I could become a social worker, but can't afford to. I could become a paediatrician, but I wouldn't want to train for all those years. I'm locked – yes, irrevocably – into the sort of job I'm doing now. The only thing I can really change is where I do it. And I really like Devon. Even our rush-hour traffic jams allow you to look at lovely scenery.'

My God, he hadn't noticed that tailback, had he? Breaking hard, he joined the queue for the A38.

Two empty juice glasses, two plates, two mugs – fancy Beth having a bloke stay overnight. Emma picked up her toast and carried it through to Beth's bedroom. Stupid cow, thinking that if she made the bed nicely it wouldn't give the game away, when there was all that evidence in the dishwasher. Look at that dressing table – she must spend a fortune on cosmetics. Emma parked the toast on the edge and picked up some of the bottles. Skin care: Christian Dior, Helena Rubenstein – oh, yes, Beth was fighting wrinkles all right.

Well, she didn't look too bad for her age. So who was this bloke? Must have been Christopher Starling. But there'd been no BMW around when Conrad had brought her home last night. And she hadn't heard one arrive later. She must have gone out like a light.

She peered at herself in the mirror. The glands seemed to have gone down altogether now. Not that they'd ever been as big as they felt, which was like tennis balls. A bit of swelling under the jaw, that was all. And now even that was gone. The trouble was, she'd need a new sick note next week, or she'd have to go back to work. And that meant going back to bloody Coventry.

She sat on the bed. Was she sure enough of Conrad to get him to come back up there? Or to ask for a transfer down here? No. Not until they'd been to bed together. And even then – well, she didn't see him whizzing up and down to the Midlands, not with a farm to run. Maybe it was time to show a bit more interest in the farm. If he had a farm shop she could always get him to sack one of the assistants and put her in instead. Yes, that sounded OK. Better still if she offered to work there and he said no, he was earning enough for both of them.

But – as he kept saying – it was early days yet. So what she had to do was make sure she stayed down here. With Beth.

Well, Beth was out so much she didn't seem to have time to nag, so that wasn't a problem. Especially when she could spend her evenings with Conrad. And maybe start spending her nights there too.

But to do that she had to get a sick note or risk the sack.

She picked up the toast – it was cold now – and wandered back into the kitchen. She'd better put it in that bin thing Beth kept by the sink for her compost heap. God, it was so gross, putting all this stuff in a bin in the garden. Recycling. Think of that utility room – bottles here, paper there. And now there was a special little carrier bag for Emma's cans:

no, she wasn't even allowed to chuck her own cans in the dustbin. Funny thing was, Conrad seemed to think it was a good idea – he even carried empty ones for her rather than let her stick them in a street bin.

She shoved more bread into the toaster and thought about that sick note. If Mum and Dad were home, there'd be no problem – she could get Mum to phone the surgery and tell the receptionist to leave one for Dad to collect. If she tried it, the old cow would tell her she had to make an appointment. Even if it meant driving two hundred miles to see the doctor. Never mind, she could always get Beth to phone. Beth could be bossy when she wanted. God, and how!

Now what?

'What brought you to Devon?' Beth asked, as the traffic trickled forward. 'I really am sorry about this – taking your time . . .'

'It's fine, Beth. It's what friends do, right?'

Yes! That sounded so good. It was so good having a friend she could say anything to. Oh, she had friends from the past, but it was difficult to whinge when you were out-earning them by so much and they had families to support on their pittances. And it was hard for heads to hobnob with teachers over whom they had such power. Not just hiring and firing, but over discipline and budget and – yes – pay.

'Right,' she agreed.

'Like you . . . like you keeping quiet about me . . .'

The poor man was writhing with embarrassment.

She hoped he felt the kindness behind her smile. In case he didn't, she reached for the hand resting on the gear lever and squeezed it lightly. 'How are you going to tackle telling her? All in one fell swoop? Or bit by bit? That might be better.'

He turned to her as if she'd said something brilliant. She returned her hand to her lap, folding it under the other.

'You mean . . . ?'

'Well, take her to your house. There must be some bits that don't give you away. Keep her to those. She surely wouldn't expect a conducted tour, not if you'd just taken her round for coffee.'

He had his eyes on the road again. 'The house is a bit of a giveaway.' He told her all about it.

His face gave him away with every sentence he spoke. If you only had to see him looking at Emma to see how much he fancied her, a glance would betray his utter love for Tucker's Hay. But a puzzled, confused love: the setting, the building, the contents – he glowed when he spoke of them. It was as if he were pressing them to his heart, even as he inched the car forward. So what was missing? Why the puzzled frown?

'And I'm very well looked after,' he said, with a grin. 'Terry does all the maintenance – house and garden. He's brilliant. And his wife – Marie – she's the most wonderful cook. Only problem is, she's pregnant. But I've bought a big American freezer and she's filling it with all sorts of meals for one. So I shan't starve while she's on maternity leave.'

'What'll happen to the baby when she comes back?'

'Oh, that's no problem. We've set up one of the rooms as its nursery – nice and bright and sunny. And it can have a playpen in the kitchen, later on.'

Poor man. OK, what a wonderful employer, but so desperate for a cook. Or was it simply a cook he needed? Wasn't Marie rather more than that – well, Marie and Terry? Other human beings around the place? Was that Conrad's problem with Tucker's Hay?

Should she risk it? Well, she'd opened up to him, and it sounded as if he needed a similar opportunity.

'It sounds as if you're in quite a remote place?'

He snorted. 'Yes; I forgot that splendid isolation can involve being . . .' He turned to her. 'Who was it said that?'

'Some Canadian politician. And then a British one borrowed it.'

'I'll look it up.' He shifted in his seat. 'I don't want my dad to know about this, Beth. He thinks Tucker's Hay's the best thing since sliced bread. He's so proud of me. He'd be so sad if he so much as sniffed any regrets. I don't want to let him down. He's a great guy. Used to be a teacher – retired now, of course. You two will get along great guns.'

'I can't wait to meet him,' she said, meaning it. 'Or,' she added, 'to see Tucker's Hay. Tell you what,' she added, laughing as kindly as she could, 'when I come, I'll bring you a house-warming present – a basic cook-book. Delia or someone. Turn left here – and gird yourself for the real traffic battle.'

Twelve

B eth got home to find Emma sitting – no, reclining – on the sofa. That dressing gown was either a wonderful success or a total disaster, depending on whether you wanted to please your niece or you were embarrassed by the amount of naked flesh she chose to reveal to the world.

'No Conrad?' she asked. It would have been nice to continue the morning's exchange of confidences. No, they couldn't have done, could they? – not with Emma around.

'No. No, I got a bit tired,' Emma added, after a pause. She fumbled for the zapper and reduced the TV sound a micro-decibel. 'So he brought me home and went back to his place to do some work, he said.'

Beth hung up her coat and brought through a glass of wine for herself and a coke for Emma. 'Have you eaten or shall I order a pizza?'

'Don't fancy another pizza. Had one for lunch. Oh, there don't seem to be any left.'

Well, Beth told herself, that wasn't a problem. Not really. It was about time for a big supermarket shop. Beth always used the local shops when she could – some of them even delivered, bless them – but there were things they couldn't provide: pizzas with her favourite toppings, for instance.

'What else might you fancy?'

'I'd kill for a McDonald's.'

'There is a burger place in the town – but it'll be closed by now.' Dawlish was at its fast-food best during the holiday season. 'And I've no idea where the nearest McDonald's is.

There's the Indian and Chinese – we could eat in or out. And several chippies. No?'

Emma shook her head. It was only now Beth realised that Emma might have been crying. She sat down beside her. 'Are you sure you're all right, love?'

Emma sniffed.

Beth passed tissues. 'What is it, love?'

And now the tears came in earnest. 'I've had such a boring day. And Conrad showed me this tip of a stately home. All these dark panels. And I've got to go back to Coventry to the doctor's – my sick note!' she wailed.

All too aware that Emma's return to work was exactly what she'd been praying for, Beth said, 'And you're not up to work, yet?'

'Oh, Beth, it's so horrible. You've no idea how bad it is there. I'm so bored and there are all these dreadful people complaining.'

Beth swallowed. Now wasn't the time to remind Emma that she'd warned her against leaving school at sixteen with only GCSEs. The girl was bright enough to have done A levels, either at school or at college. Or there were less academic, more practical ways to qualifications, more, Beth would have thought, to Emma's taste. She'd thought at one time her counsels might have prevailed, but Sylvia had insisted on A levels or nothing – and the latter was what she'd got.

'Is it work or your glands that are horrible?' she asked gently.

'Both!'

'Well, if you're still poorly, I'm sure your GP will sign you off a bit longer. But if you want another job, it's much easier to get one while you're employed. New employers would look at any gaps in your employment history and ask questions. And hearing that you've had glandular fever is an answer they might not like. So I do think we've got to keep your present employer happy. Sick note it'll have to be.'

'But how on earth do I get one? I mean, Mummy and

Daddy . . . the house'll be all cold and I shall have to go on the coach and I'm always sick.'

'I'm sure there's a train service, even if you have to change. But I could always have a word with the local surgery – see if one of the doctors there would be allowed to see you and issue a note. I've an idea, though, that if you're not on their list, they're only supposed to see you if you're an emergency. Leave it to me, anyway. I suppose,' she added slowly, 'if they can't see you, we'll have to find a way of getting you to Leicester.' Which meant at least a day off work. Unless Conrad could be persuaded to do the honours before he went to the States. 'Now, what about some food?'

Emma managed a weak smile: 'D'you remember that soup you used to make that time I had the bad teeth?'

Emma lay back in bed, smiling at the ceiling. Things weren't going so badly. Oh, she'd hated that farmhouse place that Conrad had taken her to, but she was sure she could persuade him to find somewhere nicer. Not that she'd say anything yet. Not until they were sleeping together – that was the time to ask, it said in that mag – when you were lying in each other's arms afterwards. It had said if you wanted to give him a really good time, you should have your tongue pierced. Well, she wouldn't mind a stud in her mouth, but she certainly didn't want to suck one of those great ugly things. It wasn't hygienic, not if you asked her. Though her girlfriends all said they'd done it. Once or twice. Maybe if the condom tasted of chocolate or strawberries it wouldn't be so bad. She'd have to think about it.

Meanwhile all she had to do was persuade Beth's doctor that she was still too ill to work. That soup had been a really good idea. Apart from anything else it kept Beth in the kitchen for half an hour so she could watch TV in peace with no disapproving sighs from the corner. And then not eating it: that had really convinced Beth that she was poorly.

She shivered. Maybe it wasn't such a good idea practising

91

sleeping without a nightie till she'd got a nice warm man in bed beside her.

Beth was so tired she went straight to bed. And was still as wide awake as she could be after an hour. There was no doubt that there had been toast crumbs on her dressing table. She certainly hadn't put her breakfast down there. Nor had Conrad. So it didn't take massive powers of deduction to realise that Emma had been in her room. Her room. Well, perhaps the girl had run out of tampons or tissues or something. She mustn't jump to silly conclusions. In any case, what conclusions were there to draw? None except that Emma had been in there. None.

But she didn't like it. No, she really didn't like the thought of someone else – anyone else – poking round her things.

At last Beth thought about Conrad's suggestion last night. Why not have a warm bath with a generous dollop of some exotic oil? It wasn't as if she didn't have enough to choose from. But even as she slipped her dressing gown on she remembered that the room the far side of the bathroom was Emma's, and that Emma needed her sleep. Why not do as she always did – look for something to occupy her time? She hadn't even checked today's post.

She gathered it from the kitchen – a couple of bills, yes, and a couple of letters, two of them from abroad. One was from her Canadian cousin, the one whose husband was battering her – not the sort of letter to leave lying round where other eyes could read it. She took them straight up to her office. Her refuge. To find, of course, the sofa bed still in bed mode. Conrad hadn't had time, had he, to strip it and fold the bedclothes? He'd been trying to get her to work on time. What a nice man he was. She hoped she'd meet his father – he'd certainly done a good job on him. She smoothed the pillows absently. What a shame Emma was too ill for them even to kiss! Except that she wasn't, of course. It was just male cowardice. Look at the way Richard had wanted nursing when he had so much as a sniffle but never came near her when she had had that dreadful flu. Ah, but at that time he'd had a completely different reason to stay away.

She tucked the personal letters into a folder, and the bills in her household file – they were only confirming deductions by direct debit. On impulse she locked both in the filing cabinet. Only then did she remember she shouldn't have been walking round – it must seem to Emma as if she were stamping on her head.

So what stately home had Conrad taken Emma to? It was very foolish of him to drag her round one of those places where you could walk miles and never notice how tired you – or your girlfriend – were getting. She ran the local ones round her mind – couldn't think of any that opened before Easter. My God! He'd taken her to Tucker's Hay, hadn't he? And Emma had succumbed to fatigue and almost certainly whininess. She'd always been an embarrassment in such situations when she was a child: she probably hadn't grown out of it yet. What would she have said about it to mortify the poor man? *All those dark panels . . .* She hadn't mentioned a pig, so poor Conrad couldn't have dared risk introducing them. Poor, poor man, having the home of his dreams rubbished by presumably the woman of his dreams. It was a pity it was so late: she would have phoned to offer – offer what?

It was cold up here now the heating had switched itself off. She could have done with a thick dressing gown and slippers, not one that was a more expensive version of Emma's, bought at a time when sexy lingerie had been appropriate. On impulse, she slipped under the duvet and reach – automatically – for the light. How long had it been since the spare bed was her only refuge? She shuddered. Not long enough. But at least in her present home, every bed was her own. Or had been till the advent of Emma.

'Gutted, Falstaff. Gutted. That's how I feel. She didn't even like my kitchen! Hated the hall. She didn't say anything.

Didn't have to. Just stood there and looked. As if she was on some trip to a National Trust place, and she couldn't wait to get to the shop and the café. Well, she liked the tea and cake. Marie did me proud. But she never asked how I'd come by such good cakes. Not once. Just took them and ate them.' He reached down for Falstaff's ears. 'At least you're grateful when I feed you. Not that I want her to be grateful. No, of course I don't. Isn't that the point of all this incognito stuff? So she loves me, not my reputation. Right? Beth's quick enough to twig – you know, she even made me put on shades when I dropped her off this morning. Some comment about not all kids being as musically challenged as Emma. And something about staff morale if the teachers saw her swanning up in a big car driven by a handsome man.'

Falstaff grunted.

'Yes, she's a nice woman. I thought she must be some sort of power freak at first. But the better I know her, the less I feel that. I wish I could talk to her about Emma and this afternoon.'

Falstaff snuffled and banged his trough.

'Sorry, mate. You really have had enough for today. If you get too fat you won't be able to mate, you know. The sows won't fancy you.'

Except they did, didn't they? Look at those elephant seals on TV the other week – the females slavering for the biggest lumps of blubber.

'Ah! Schmoozing up to me again, are you? Well, I just happen to have one last apple . . . I suppose I could always phone her. But what if Emma answered the phone? That wouldn't go down very well – me wanting to talk to her aunt. No, she wouldn't: she knows I always call her on her mobile. But what if Beth gave the game away? "Hello, Conrad!" or something.' But he shook his head. Beth had more presence of mind than that.

He scratched the proffered ear one last time and headed back to the house. He'd told Emma he had to work, and it was true. There was a whole batch of e-mails from the States about the tour, for one thing. If he got those out of the way, it would be late enough to phone Beth without any fear of Emma still being awake.

He looked at his watch. Surely he hadn't been busy all that time? But he must have been. Well, that was it, wasn't it. He couldn't possibly phone even Beth at this time of night. Jesus! He'd not even tidied his bed away from her office. Yet another job for the poor woman to fit in. He'd take her some flowers tomorrow to say thank you.

Or would he? For some reason he'd said nothing about his overnight stay to Emma. And he had the strangest suspicion that Beth wouldn't have either.

Thirteen

What did it matter if you couldn't get the pizzas you wanted when you could buy organic meat, fish and vegetables and delectable home-cooked flans from local shopkeepers who'd become your friends? And the walk was good for her. Two walks, in fact – you didn't attempt to carry too heavy a load up her hill! It would have been good if she could have persuaded Emma to indulge in some gentle exercise, but it was quite obvious she didn't want to. The girl had even offered to peg the first load of washing on the line and load the washing machine a second time. Presumably she'd spend the rest of the morning titivating herself for Conrad, who – she'd casually let slip – would be taking her out for lunch.

Beth paused halfway back down Queen Street to shift her grip on her shopping bags. There were vases crammed full of early pinks outside the florist-cum-greengrocers. They glowed in the bright sun. No. She wouldn't even try to resist. Nor the carnations that would tone perfectly with them.

'Lovely spring day like this, it does you good to treat yourself,' Sandra grinned, as she wrapped them.

Beth nodded. 'Especially to something non-fattening . . .' But her heart wasn't in it. She suddenly wished – wished as she hadn't wished for years – that someone might care enough to treat her. But she pulled herself up short. Christopher Starling would buy her armfuls of flowers if she were to so much as hint at a desire for some. He'd probably be offended, somewhere deep in his soul, that she'd had to buy such a treat for herself: wasn't that what gentlemen were for? To buy flowers for ladies? She could almost guarantee something extravagant from Interflora to celebrate the first time they slept together.

Which would, Beth, be when? Was she simply waiting for Emma to leave? or was she holding back for some other reason? The business of the tenders, for instance. She was still unhappy at having been asked to do something as suspect as that. And unhappy at having acquiesced. The problem took her all the way back up the long hill to the lane to her bungalow. She stopped two or three times to chat to neighbours and admire spring gardens, and then struck off – the last pull always threatened to defeat her – on her own.

The front door was locked. What on earth was Emma doing? No one locked doors round here – older locals had left them unlocked even when they went shopping, until town-raised burglars with no conception of neighbourly honesty had forced them to change their ways. Shrugging, she let herself in, calling as she went though to the kitchen. No response. Conrad must have arrived to take her out earlier than planned. Which was a shame: it would have been useful to synchronise their versions of the night before.

Ah. The first load of shopping sat unpacked where she'd dumped it. A pile of washing still lay on the floor and the machine was still full. Well, no problem. After all, she always had to peg out her own washing. Except that most of this was Emma's. How did she manage to get through so many clothes, when all she did was mope around all day? Never mind, with a brisk wind like this, everything should soon be dry.

It didn't take long to put the shopping away, either, and she'd managed to get in a good hour's work in her study before she allowed herself a coffee.

She was just taking a mug back upstairs when the front doorbell rang.

'Conrad!'

'Hi. Hope I'm not too early.' He looked meaningfully at the spare bedroom. Emma's bedroom.

Shaking her head, Beth stepped back to let him in. 'There's no sign of her,' she said, shutting the door. 'I thought you must already have collected her.' She realised she was still holding the untouched coffee. 'Fancy a cup?'

'Love one. Hang on, I'll get it. You go and sit down.'

Go and sit down! It made her sound about ninety! She wandered into the kitchen and sat down at the table while he filled the kettle. He laughed: 'I'm quite capable, you know.' But the laugh became awkward, embarrassed. 'Beth – about the other night . . .'

'When you slept in my spare bed? No, I didn't need to tell Emma that – not when she can be so . . . so . . . emotional,' she concluded, with more desperation than she hoped she showed. Being unkind about Emma to Emma's boyfriend was unacceptable.

To her relief he laughed again. 'Yes. Sometimes. And of course, it's so bad for her – brings up her glands before you can say knife. Anyway – thanks.' He turned his attention to the coffee, stirring it rather more than she thought necessary.

Should she mention Emma's visit to his house or wait for him to broach the subject? To fill a growing silence, she asked, 'Have you had a conducted tour of my estate, yet, Conrad? The spring bulbs are looking good. And – yes, I think the machine's spun itself to sleep – I can hang the washing out while you inspect the pots on the patio!'

Perhaps she wasn't surprised when he started feeling the washing already on the line. He said seriously, 'I think these shirts are about right for ironing, if you like them a bit on the damp side. Then there'd be room for that sheet, wouldn't there?'

'Someone got you beautifully domesticated,' she said, hoping she sounded neither sexist nor nosy.

'My dad,' he said promptly. 'Who was Mum and Dad to me actually. Mum died when I was small. Road accident. So

Dad taught at this big comp during the day and looked after me all the rest of the time. God knows how he managed. I think,' he added, 'maybe schools were less pressured than they are now. No National Curriculum. He's retired now. He's off seeing his sister in Australia at the moment.'

'You miss him?' It was hardly a question, more a prompt.

For reply he shook out a duvet cover and pegged it up.

'He's my best mate,' he said at last. 'You'll like him. Don't know about Emma, though.'

Or did he mean, he didn't know whether his father would approve of Emma?

'She's very young,' she began gently, and then stopped abruptly. The man must be all too aware of the age gap, mustn't he? And she suspected that, while the glandular fever provided an excellent reason for delaying, some of his hesitation might well lie elsewhere.

She reached for the pillow cases. Look at the way the sun caught his ruffled hair! And how the bedlinen reflected sunlight back on to his face as if it were a clever photographer's lighting effect. No wonder if young women had thrust themselves at him – either because of his looks or because of his superstar status. And – she wished the next thought had stayed at the back of her mind – he'd slept with some of them.

'Very young,' he echoed sadly, at last. 'But have you ever seen a more beautiful . . .' His voice tailed off. He managed an amused laugh. 'I suppose with your job you've seen dozens.'

'Quite a few as beautiful,' she said. 'None more.' But very many who were more attractive, because of their intelligence, kindness, sense of humour . . .

He didn't seem to look beneath her answer, but nodded, as if somehow reassured.

'The least I can do,' he said, as they came back into the house, 'is let me tidy up your study. I should have done it the other morning. I mean, this is a smashing drying day

– we'd get your sheets dry and aired before you can say March winds.'

'Or indeed April showers. No, there's no need. I can—'

'You can do an awful lot, Beth, but you can't do everything. I'll have a word with Emma – get her to pull her weight a bit more.'

'How about a deal? I let you strip your bed if you promise to say nothing?' How did she dare ask a besotted lover anything like that? But the words were out.

'Done,' he said, suddenly dodging in front of her up her stairs. 'Hey, this is even nicer by daylight! Look at that sky! Oh, and the sea over there! And – my God – all these books.' He ran his finger along some of the shelves. 'Archaeology; art; music; poetry; philosophy . . .'

'Mostly philosophy of education,' she demurred.

'Even so. And all these lovely textures!' He touched the wood of the ceiling, the floor, felt with thumb and forefinger one of her rugs. Then, suddenly, he said, 'Look . . . I know you were coming up here to work when I arrived. Do you mind if I just sit and read while I wait? Up here? It's so . . .'

'No problem,' she said, wondering why on earth a woman who loved her privacy so much would say such a stupid thing, and gathering up the sheets. 'I'll just pop these in the machine. Do you want me to bring up the paper? Or do you want to browse?'

For all he was supposed to be reading the *Guardian* Weekend section, Conrad couldn't help letting his eyes roam round the room. In the spring light, it seemed to glow. It was like being inside a deep-throated daffodil. He could have stayed there all day. And then he was on his feet. Where on earth could Emma be? He'd been messing round when he should have been out searching the streets of Dawlish for her. What if she'd had a blackout? Some sort of accident? And why had the panic taken till this moment to arrive?

Beth was looking at him with concern. Before he could

say anything, she murmured, 'You know, I think all things being equal it might be better if she found you pacing round in anxiety downstairs, not sitting enjoying yourself up here. I'll be down in a couple of minutes.'

He hesitated.

'Didn't you hear the gate? Go!'

Abandoning the paper, he ran as fast as he could down the staircase. Bloody ears letting him down again. The specialist had warned him about premature loss on some frequencies – all that standing round in front of huge amplifiers belting out decibels of sound. Good job Beth had all her faculties: God, that woman missed nothing, did she? Except how like her niece she was. And there was Emma now, opening the front door.

She almost fell into his arms.

'My darling, where've you been?' he demanded. 'I didn't know where to start looking . . .' It was impossible to continue – not with those sharp ears upstairs. Not that she'd be spying, not Beth; but she'd know exactly how worried he hadn't been. To silence her amusement as much as his hypocrisy, he did what he knew would please Emma best. He bent and kissed her.

After all that fuss, why on earth had he decided to kiss her now? But he kissed very nicely, and Emma was going to kiss him back, with interest. Both hands pressing his back, she rubbed herself against his crotch. And then slipped a hand down to his bum, pulling it hard against her. Time for her tongue to go in? Yes, that would encourage him to do the same. Oh, yes. Oh, yes. And judging by the state of his . . . his, well, his penis, it wouldn't be long before she could persuade him into bed.

But he pushed her away. Not quickly, but firmly. When she took his hand and pulled him towards her bedroom, he only shook his head.

'Why ever not? I'm on the pill.'

He put his finger to his lips. 'Beth!' he mouthed, pointing upwards.

'She won't mind!' She pulled more urgently. Then she remembered what she'd had to do with Jase. She put her hand on the front of his trousers and squeezed the bulge.

This time he grabbed her wrist. 'Emma! For Christ's sake.' He looked really wild for a moment. Not with desire, either. Next thing she knew he was pulling her – quite roughly – into the kitchen. He shut the door, leaning on it. Ah, so he did want her. Emma tried again.

This time he took both wrists and pushed her away from him till she had to sit down. 'Darling Em,' he was saying, 'you know how I want you. But not here. Not now. Not when B— Not when your aunt would hear everything we said. That's not how I want it. I want our first time to be . . . special.'

All she'd been through this morning finally hit her and she burst into tears. Real ones. Even if some of them were tears of anger.

'My darling!' Yes, he took her in his arms, and rocked her backwards and forwards. But he kissed her hair, not her face. 'I didn't mean . . . I wanted . . .'

She pushed him away, smearing away the tears with the heel of her hand. 'And there I spent the whole morning trying to do something really nice for you. Only when I found a place, right over in Newton Abbot, he said he wouldn't do it, not without proof of my age.'

'What on earth did you . . . ?'

She smiled, licking her lips and then widening the smile to show her tongue. 'I thought you'd like it,' she said, 'if I had this pierced.' She waggled the tip at him.

'Em,' he said, looking as if he hadn't understood, 'why on earth . . . ?'

'Because,' she said, 'it said in this magazine that girls ought to have it done for when they fell— when they fallope— when they sucked you off,' she concluded, all of a rush. 'Only if I do, I know I'm on the pill but you'll have to wear a condom.'

*   *   *

102

Burying her face in her hands Beth ran back upstairs. Oh God, talk about conversations better not overheard. Poor Emma. Expecting to find a body-piercer in Dawlish. And only so that she could offer Conrad fellatio. And not knowing the right word. Not that anyone used it, surely! It wasn't until she'd shut herself in her study and sunk on to the sofa that she dared let the laughter come.

Except that it wasn't funny, was it? There was in fact something decidedly unfunny about the whole thing. Her niece sucking off Conrad in her house. Come to think of it, she didn't want Emma and Conrad having any sort of sex in her house. Conrad at least had realised that – she'd overheard him trying to put Emma off. She'd shut the door on that conversation, too. She'd only come down because she'd heard a door close and thought it might be the front one. If she'd known they were in the kitchen, she'd have stayed put. Only then she wouldn't have had the glorious experience of hearing Emma offer Conrad a sexual delight she couldn't even pronounce.

Beth lay back on the sofa bed and laughed. Laughed till the tears came and she found she couldn't stop – either the laughter or the tears.

Fourteen

'Cockwood,' Beth repeated, still straight-faced. But it wouldn't be too long before it cracked, would it? 'It's a very good pub.'

Conrad nodded, his mock solemnity matching hers.

'But you don't have to show us the way. Conrad must have a map,' Emma said.

He held his breath and counted. He needed a third party present. Someone to carry the conversation while he worked out exactly what to do and say. The 'do' part was easy. Nothing. Not yet. Much as he wanted to make love to her, he had to back off. Just till he came back from the States. Just to give her breathing space. Just so she'd know what she was doing. As if he wanted her to – my God, what was the word she'd been looking for? – fellate him? Well, of course he'd like her to have him in her mouth, but not yet. Not until she knew – exactly – what she was doing. The 'say' part was the tricky one. He'd got to find the right words – and the right tone to say them in – to tell her it wasn't because he didn't love her that he wasn't taking her to bed, but because he did. OK, it was old-fashioned. But it was time for her to work out if she was sure. By the time she was thirty, he'd be fifty. (My God, wasn't that out of some play? Shaw?) Because it wasn't just a great fuck he wanted, it was a lasting relationship, full of trust and respect.

'Look,' he tried again, 'it's lunchtime. We all need lunch. Beth knows a good place to have lunch. Let's just get in my car and go and have lunch.' He sought and found Beth's eyes, which looked, now he came to think of it, a bit puffy. She must have been asleep.

She gave him the tiniest nod.

'I have to be back by two,' she said, almost as if begrudging the time.

'OK! Time to move, then. You're sure you'll be warm enough, darling?'

'I don't suppose there's time for me to change.'

'Plenty of time for you to get that pretty jacket.'

As Emma left the kitchen, Beth's face cracked. Just as he'd predicted. But she was angry as well as amused, wasn't she?

'One of these days,' she said, fighting for control, 'you can tell me exactly what's going on.'

He looked at her steadily. Somehow he didn't think he ever would. And he hoped she'd never ask again. Using people wasn't something he liked to admit to. But it wasn't just that. He'd have felt bad about treating Emma to a good meal knowing that Beth would be on her own. In fact, he'd felt bad about it right from the first evening. It wasn't that he was afraid Beth couldn't manage. Beth could manage anything. He had an idea that she'd be a very good cook. And she clearly was used to a singleton's life. It was just that – no, she didn't ever look anything like forlorn. It was more that he felt she ought to, perhaps. No, the only time he'd seen her in less than control was the first evening. And anyone could look gobsmacked after news like she'd had. Except that it wasn't gobsmacked; it was vulnerable.

She didn't look vulnerable now. Just, to be honest, very attractive: jeans and sweaters suited her as much as those nifty suits. Unlike most tall women, she carried herself proud, no hint of a droop. She could give Emma a few lessons in skin care. Well, persuade her not to smoke – that'd be a help. So why should he think her vulnerable? Emma had gossiped away about Beth's past – apparently she'd had a very attractive boyfriend, who'd created a terrible scandal. Scandals were rare enough these days, real scandals, not just nine-day media wonders. But she'd been very unclear about details. Either Beth and Emma's parents had kept things from her, or she really was respecting the promise of privacy she said Beth had extracted. He rather hoped it was the latter.

The clouds were already coming down as they set off for the tiny pub overlooking the little harbour of Cockwood – both those in the sky and those over Emma's face. Beth had firmly established herself as a back-seat navigator – not that there was much to do in the way of guiding – leaving the front passenger seat without argument to Emma. But she was far from welcome. And she could quite understand. In Emma's place, she wouldn't have wanted an – elderly! – aunt playing gooseberry. Any more than in Conrad's place she'd have wanted one. What was he up to? Was he having second thoughts? No – he didn't look at Emma as if anything except love filled his thoughts.

'Turn right here,' she said crisply.

No, there was something besides love, wasn't there? Love and . . . pain? There was something amiss, wasn't there? She had the oddest feeling that though she would bet her pension that Emma would regard her as the last person in the world to confide in, Conrad would feel that – after his father – she was the first. She wasn't at all sure, however, that she wanted to act as his counsellor. She wanted to be his friend – in this relaxed, easy relationship they'd suddenly fallen into. She'd love to talk over the Christopher Starling business. But perhaps he'd welcome details of her relationships no more than she'd welcome details of his. Of course, the circumstances were completely different, weren't they?

'Follow the road round to the left.'

After all, she could talk about the fire and the paper tenders as a completely abstract issue. It didn't involve anyone he knew. Not like any discussions about Emma.

'There's a tiny car park just beyond the pub – there, on the left.'

He slowed right down. 'Why didn't I get a smaller car? OK. I'll back in. Much safer.'

* * *

It was all dark and nasty. A really poky little place. Why on earth had Beth raved about it? So the view across the harbour was supposed to be magic. Well, good for it. You couldn't even see the harbour from where she was sitting. And in any case, the tide was out and there was nothing but a few boats lying in the mud. And it was all very well for Beth and Conrad to rabbit on about the fish but hers had come full of nasty little bones. And they were talking about music, for goodness' sake. It seemed they'd both been to some concert in Exeter – listen to them.

'But that pianist,' Conrad was saying, 'was so self-indulgent. That slow movement was all over the place. *Rubato*! He practically rubbed it out!'

Beth was giggling like one of her own stupid pupils as if he'd made a really funny joke.

'You know,' Conrad continued, leaning forward, 'I nearly got up and said, "Hang on, I could do better than that!" I mean—'

'Exactly,' Beth interrupted him.

Why had she interrupted like that? And why did she and Conrad exchange that quick smile when they thought she wasn't looking? No, they couldn't have done. Beth was holding forth about the last concert she'd been to at the University and Conrad had reached under the table as she'd always wanted him to do and taken her hand. Wouldn't it be great to walk into Boots holding his hand like that and give in her notice? The expression on the other girls' faces would be worth framing. OK, he was a bit old, but when they saw how nice-looking he was and his clothes and his car . . . No, she'd keep quiet about that awful house – wait till she'd made him get somewhere nicer, with one of those digital TVs. A nice big screen in the corner of their living room.

The others didn't want a pudding till she pointed out the ice cream on the menu blackboard. Oh, dear. Why had she bothered? There they were, dying to try it. All this organic business. And then, when it came, Beth kept clapping her hand to her mouth and Conrad started talking about some toothpaste, of all things. Well, her teeth were all right, and she might just have another portion. That would teach Beth to slide glances at her watch when she thought no one was looking. If she'd wheedled an invitation, she could bloody well stay put until Emma had finished.

'More?' Beth exclaimed, but nodded at the waitress, who went off. 'Your teeth must be in better condition than mine! But it was superb, wasn't it? Wonderfully creamy and the taste went on for ever.'

Conrad laughed. 'Trouble is, the calories stick on for ever.' He patted his stomach. 'Look at Emma: willow-thin despite all she puts away.'

Emma smiled up at him. He took her hand and kissed it.

She was too busy eating the next bowl of ice cream to take much notice of what they were talking about next, but she picked up something about paper. Beth had dropped her voice so low that Conrad had to lean right forward to hear what she was saying. He looked very serious. Suddenly Beth put a finger to her lips. And Conrad only reached across the table and took her hand. Beth's hand! 'We'll talk about it later,' he said. And then he was on his feet, holding out his other hand. Who to?

'Elizabeth – what a delightful surprise!'

It was that bloke of Beth's. The one with the Beamer. Emma pushed away her dish, mopping her lips daintily on the paper serviette.

Beth kept her cool. 'Christopher – I'd like you to meet Conrad. Conrad – Christopher Starling. And you remember Emma, my niece.'

Oh, yes – he remembered her all right. She smiled up at him, holding out her hand to be shaken. 'Hello. It's nice to meet you again.' Mummy would have been proud of her.

Starling smiled – not quite uncle to favourite niece. There was an extra flicker in his eye she didn't think Beth or Conrad would have seen. And she rather wished she hadn't. Starling leaned on the back of the empty chair: he was waiting to be asked to sit down, wasn't he? But an afternoon nattering to an old lech who was sleeping with Beth wasn't her idea of fun. And it wasn't Conrad's either. He was looking at his watch and coughing apologetically. So was Beth. As if all three of them were going to leave together. Oh, no – surely Starling could take Beth. They'd like to have the house to themselves – no need to creep in late at night and flit off before Emma was even awake. Some of her mates thought it disgusting for old people to – to go to bed together. But Emma prided herself on being broad-minded. If Beth and the old guy wanted to do . . . that, well, who was she to object? Except that it was pretty gross, wasn't it?

Fifteen

'And now,' Christopher said, swirling his after-dinner brandy around the huge balloon, 'I suppose you have to dash off home to make sure your niece is all right. Protect her from her boyfriend. Though I have to tell you, Elizabeth, that if either of them needed protecting I'd say it was him, not her.'

Beth smiled, sipping the last of her mineral water. She wanted to be stone-cold sober to tackle the hired Fiesta's lights and heater. 'Why would you say that, Christopher?'

'Don't you remember that T-shirt? I tell you, it comes to haunt me in the depths of the night! My daughters used to wear exactly the same sort of garment and never understood why I asked them not to wander round the house like that when I had guests.'

'I went out and bought her a dressing gown,' Beth admitted. 'I didn't want to get her anything frumpish: she might have taken against it and refused to wear it – you know what teenage girls are like! But I seem to have gone too far the other way!'

'Oh, I do indeed! One day,' he added, dropping his voice, 'I'd like to see you in your dressing gown. And out of it. Oh, Elizabeth, when are we . . . I did hope, you know, that this afternoon I could have run you home and we could have . . .'

Beth shook her head. 'I had so much work to do. Not to mention picking up the car from Teignmouth.'

'I can't understand why you should want one when your

110

own should be ready this week,' he said pettishly. 'And a Fiesta, for goodness' sake.'

It would have been easy to flare up: it was none of his business. But she said what she'd said to Conrad, when he'd made much the same point. 'Public transport's fine during the day, but not much fun in the evenings. Besides, when garages promise you your car and when they deliver it aren't necessarily one and the same. And it's a pleasant little car.'

If anything, his frown deepened. 'If only I'd known, nothing would have given me more pleasure than to take you to collect it.'

'It was only three or four miles out of Conrad's way. And I had to get stuck into those statistics. I . . . I shouldn't really have come out with you this evening but . . .' No, she didn't want to commit herself. She added lightly, 'I never realised Conrad had a passion for football. But I'd have expected you to share it. Come on, confess – weren't you glued to the TV this afternoon?'

That had been Conrad's excuse for providing her transport. It had seemed quite logical at the time, but now she had to admit it must have seemed simply perverse. She'd enjoyed the sight of both faces: Emma's and Christopher's. But Conrad had been insistent. He'd teased Emma for not knowing who the Sky Blues were, despite having been born and bred in Coventry. It had all been very good-humoured, even his popping his head round her study door to make sure the noise from the TV wasn't disturbing her. But she had a grain of suspicion that there was something else there. That he didn't want her to have to spend time alone with Starling unless she wanted to. He'd raised an eyebrow when Beth agreed to dine with Starling that evening, but had guaranteed her early return by confessing very publicly that he hated to leave Emma in the house on her own. It was almost as if he divined her reluctance to do what should be so natural – to sleep with Christopher.

'I'm a rugby man myself,' Christopher smiled. 'But whatever the game was, I'd rather have spent the afternoon with a beautiful woman than staring at the TV. I'd have thought . . . he and Emma?' He coughed delicately.

So, of course, would Beth. There was Conrad's fear of illness, of course, but surely there was something else. But she wasn't about to chew the matter over with Starling. 'I don't think so,' she said simply. 'Not that it's any of my business, of course. That was a lovely meal, Christopher.'

'And we still have Tuesday to look forward to,' he said, lifting her hand to kiss it. 'May I offer you one last toast? To Emma's speedy return – to health and to Coventry.'

Beth raised her glass, smiling. It was time to tackle that Fiesta, wasn't it?

She could, of course, have gone back with Christopher. If Conrad had been prepared to wait till twelve for her return, he'd have been prepared to wait till one. He could even have made himself up a bed in her study again: a man like him would have had no difficulty running the airing cupboard to ground. Any more, it turned out, when she let herself quietly into the bungalow, than he'd have trouble finding the whisky.

'Come and sit; after an evening on the wagon you deserve a tipple,' he said, pouring into a glass he had ready. 'What was the car like?'

'Fine. Once I'd worked out where everything was.' But her MG it wasn't.

'Did you have a pleasant time?'

She looked at him sharply. But there was no trace of irony in his face.

'It was an excellent meal, thank you.'

His eyebrows shot up at the chill in her voice.

'If you like too much steak cooked with too many flames too close to your table,' she continued, laughing. 'And every sweet covered in cream from a can.'

'Pretty naff, then?'

'Pretty naff. And it was all so expensive, so . . . so . . . vulgar!'

'And Sparrow didn't complain?'

'Starling,' she corrected him.

'Poor man,' he said, sitting back in his corner of the sofa, one arm resting along the back, long legs stretched in front of him. 'Fancy going through life wishing you were a Red Kite.'

'No, he wouldn't want to be a red anything,' she declared.

'A Golden Eagle, then?'

'That's more like.' She sat in her favourite chair, after a moment slipping off her shoes and folding her feet under her. 'But it would be difficult to go to bed with a bird of prey.' Why on earth had she said that? It must be the whisky talking!

'You don't have much option if you want to go to bed with him.'

'Is that how you see him?'

'Don't you?'

She shook her head firmly.

'How do you see him then?'

'As a rather lonely widower whose last relationship didn't work out and who's been . . . been treading carefully in this.'

'And how do you see you?' He leaned forward, elbows on knees. As if to give her a moment to collect herself, he sipped the whisky.

'In rather the same way, perhaps,' she said cautiously. For a painful instant she saw herself as a woman who'd foolishly chosen to endure a cross-questioning when she could have spent a night in a man's uncritical arms. It was so long since she'd been gentled, caressed.

'What went wrong in your relationship?'

Her head shot up. 'What's Emma been saying?'

'Nothing, nothing. Said, in fact, she'd promised to keep your secret.'

'Which implies, of course, there is a secret.' She sat upright. 'It's none of her business. Or yours.'

'I know it isn't. I know. I just wondered . . . you know, they say talking helps.'

113

She thought back to the bleak room that officialdom had done its best to make user-friendly where she'd spent all those hours talking. The kindness, the tissues, the support – and all the time the steely determination to get at the truth. That was, after all, what the police were for.

'I'm so sorry.' He looked it.

She tried for casual, but felt herself missing by a mile. 'It's OK. You weren't to know . . . that talking . . . doesn't always help.'

The silence got deeper and deeper.

'Would you rather I went or stayed?'

It was better to avoid his gaze: she got up and collected the glasses, his empty, hers still half-full. 'It'd be . . . complicated . . . tomorrow morning, wouldn't it?'

'So it would. Yes. I'd forgotten.' Biting his lower lip, he headed for the hall.

She followed.

'You wouldn't mind just seeing me out of your drive, would you? It's so tight – and one wounded car's enough.'

'Sure. I've got to pop the Fiesta into the garage, anyway – don't want to leave it in the road overnight.' She slipped the front-door catch, following him down to his car. It was thanks to him – OK, thanks to Emma – that her drive was £2000 further away from being widened. No doubt the thought wasn't far from his mind. But instead of getting in, he suddenly put his arm round her shoulder, pulling her into a hug. It felt good, so good she kissed him lightly on the lips. Friend to friend. He said something into her ear as quiet as a kiss, squeezing her shoulders gently as he pulled away.

The car took its time to fire. What if it wouldn't start? Well, the study was there for him. But he got it moving, and pulled gently into the road.

She'd no idea how long she watched his tail-lights out of sight.

'Bacon and egg, Conrad?' Marie demanded, passing him

his first mug of coffee of the day. 'And I picked a couple of field mushrooms on the way up.'

'Wonderful,' he said, flipping over sections of the *Observer*. 'Could I have some fried bread?'

'Sure.'

Something in her voice made him look up. She was gripping the Aga towel rail, leaning over the hob.

He pushed a chair behind her, guided her into it. 'Come on. Sit down.'

'No. It's just . . . just a tiny twinge, that's all.'

'Sit. Leave all that where it is. Come on. Then I'll phone Terry. And the doctor.'

'I'm fine. They say babies do this sometimes.' She burst into tears.

He reached across her for a handful of kitchen towel. 'No need to get upset then. Come on, Marie. If you need to start your maternity leave early, that's fine. And you don't have to come back any sooner, you know.'

'But you . . .' She gripped his hand. My God, she wasn't having a proper contraction, was she? She wasn't due for several weeks yet.

'But what?' He smiled and touched her cheek. 'There are only three things that matter here, Marie, and I'm not one of them. You and the baby and Terry,' he said, when she stared at him as if he were talking Chinese. 'Are you feeling better now? Now, before I run you home, would you like to come along and see Terry Junior's rest-room? They finished painting it on Friday.' He offered her his arm, as if he were Mr Darcy escorting Elizabeth Bennet. Elizabeth Darcy, more like, if she was pregnant. Not that he saw Marie as a Jane Austen heroine. Poor thing, she'd have been one of the unmentioned Lower Orders. Not even as socially acceptable as the wretched girl that the dreadful Emma Woodhouse had taken up with.

So which heroine would *his* Emma resemble?

'It still smells of paint, of course, but – there, what do you think of it?'

He flung the door open. The morning sun had just come round far enough to show the room at its best – the yellow and white wallpaper and white paint.

'They'll be able to lay the carpet early next week. And then, when you've chosen the furniture, it can go straight in.' He felt as if he was talking to a child.

Marie nodded. 'Two of everything,' she murmured. 'So he won't feel confused. Same cot here as at home. Same toys here as at home. I must get the measurements for the curtains – this window's much bigger than at home.'

'You'll have them made up. No nonsense about trying to make them yourself. And Terry or I will hang them.'

'You? Look, Conrad, you don't have to do things like that. It's bad enough you doing all this for us' – she gestured round the room – 'and all the time off for the baby. Who's going to look after you while I'm off? That's what you pay me for.' It all came in a rush.

'I may not be here all that much,' he said. 'You know – holidays and staying with friends.'

'Oh, you won't be missing your first summer here?' She looked really distressed.

'Not all of it, don't you worry.' But he worried. What if Emma hated the place so much he had to get rid of it? Could he invite Beth up here first, to see if she could suggest ways of making it more habitable? Then he remembered: Beth might not want to come up here, not if she were still angry with him. He thought of her face. Angry? Not so much angry as hurt, surely. But he hadn't wanted to hurt her.

'. . . again?'

'I'm sorry?'

'I said, won't you be bringing your friend again? The young lady? Terry said she was ever so pretty.'

'When did Terry see her?'

'Oh, I asked him to keep an eye open – you know.'

Yes, he knew. Terry and half the village would have their eyes open.

'I'm sure I shall,' he said.

116

'Is she nice?'

'She's lovely. Emma. But she won't be coming till I'm back from the States.'

'Goodness! You're off – when is it? My mind's like a sieve, these days. They say it's the baby.'

'Last thing Tuesday.' Which was cutting things pretty fine. Still, he and the lads had done the routine times beyond count. Over and over. Like all the concerts. Over and over till you could play the gigs in the dark with your eyes closed. Which was why he'd refused to do a tour. No more tours, ever. And after this week – yes, today was Sunday, the start of a new week – no more gigs. Ever.

'And is she going with you? Oh, I used to feel so sorry for you, coming back to empty hotel rooms; and now you'll have someone to look after you. Make sure you have a clean shirt and that.'

He had to smile – the thought of Emma looking after his creature comforts! More likely he'd be looking after hers.

'But – oh, Conrad!' Marie's face crumpled. 'If you have her you won't be needing Terry and me.'

He tucked her hand under his arm and squeezed it. 'Of course I will. Whatever happens.'

But maybe not at a house on Dartmoor. My God, that would mean taking Marie away from her mother and the rest of her family just when she needed them most.

They went back to the kitchen, where the coffee stood untasted on the table, the bacon uncooked on the grill-pan.

'Come on, slip your coat on so I can run you home,' Conrad said. 'Time you had your feet up, remember.'

'But what about your breakfast?'

'I'll do it. Not as well as you, but I'll manage.'

She rubbed her face doubtfully. 'I suppose there's a fair bit in the freezer already. And that young lady – perhaps she'll help out.'

He smiled, but not this time at the thought of Emma. 'Actually,' he said, 'Beth – that's another friend of mine – has offered to help. By buying me a cookery book!'

Marie frowned. 'Isn't there some saying about fishing?'

Conrad scratched his head. '*If you give someone a fish, you feed him for a day. If you teach someone to fish, you feed him for the rest of his life.* Is that the one?'

'That's the one. Maybe she's the young lady you should go for.'

Sixteen

The phone call came just when Beth needed it. She'd been up in her study since six – remember the days when she'd thought a Sunday morning lie-in hers as of right? Not to mention a wonderful English breakfast. Today's had been packet fruit juice and – in this oasis of home-produced and -cured bacon, organic eggs and fresh-picked field mushrooms – a dry-as-dust breakfast bar. She was losing the plot, wasn't she? She balled the wrapper and hurled it into the bin.

'Dougie!' He was one of her oldest friends – yes, they must have met in Freshers' Week at Sussex. 'How are you?'

'I'm fine, and. more to the point, I'm here.'

'Here? Not Dawlish!' She must have sounded as excited as a girl. She felt it.

'Not quite. But Devon. Tom's got to take his auntie in Totnes to tea—'

'Is that the famous rich auntie?' Tom didn't have to work. Auntie provided what he always referred to as 'the loot'. For the last five years he'd shared the loot with Dougie, which meant Dougie no longer had to work either. A lot of loot, clearly.

'The same. Anyway, we thought we'd better spread the loot around a bit – take you out to lunch. Can you get to Totnes for one?'

Thank goodness for the hired Fiesta. But—

'Beth! Don't tell me I heard a hesitation!'

He was right to sound offended. Even to be offended. At least with Dougie she could be perfectly honest. But then, she couldn't be perfectly honest lest Emma overheard her:

119

she was never sure how far to trust the study soundproofing. 'You know I'd love nothing more. But my niece is staying here,' she added more soberly, 'and I've no idea what her lunch arrangements are.' So the intimate meal with old friends sharing confidences ebbed briskly away.

'Go and ask her. At a pinch, I suppose we could always accommodate her at our table too. Unless she still wears a bib and throws food around.'

'She's eighteen . . .'

'Not those ghastly metal braces!'

'Perfect teeth. Perfect skin. Perfect hair. Perfect figure.'

'And a perfect bore? No, you don't have to answer that question. Your silence once again betrays you. Go and ask her. I'll phone you back in five minutes.'

Emma was still in bed – since when had she been sleeping naked? – but awake. The idea of going out to lunch made her beam like a kid. When she heard it was with an old friend of Beth's the beam dimmed only slightly, but it returned at full strength when she heard about the presence of Tom. Beth saw no reason to spell out the relationship between the two men.

'Unless you've made arrangements with Conrad, Emma?'

Emma pulled a face. 'He said something about work. But he might have changed his mind. He might want to join us, mightn't he? Where would we be eating?'

'Totnes. It's a very pretty little town with—'

'Totnes? That's close to his farm. We could go and visit him.'

They could. But how would he react? If Emma's first visit hadn't been a notable success, would a second, particularly if she were accompanied by Beth? She temporised. 'On the way back, maybe.'

The phone rang. 'That'll be Dougie.'

They met in the Totnes restaurant Beth had suggested, the building old and secure enough it its sense of its history not to have to be twee. It could rely on heavy beams, colour-washed walls and old furniture – not the sort of antiques the rich would have passed down, but the heritage of artisans. She'd have to tell Conrad about it – she was sure it was the sort of place he'd like. There was no doubt that, for the looks of the occupants, their table was the best in the restaurant. Emma had obviously made a special effort, and looked her attractive best in shirt and jeans and one of Beth's jumpers. No one would have guessed she was too ill to work. Beth had done her best, but needed her well-cut shirt and skirt and carefully applied make-up to look respectable. Of the men, Tom, despite a relative lack of inches, was stunningly handsome, with his pale, aquiline features and dark curly hair. He was regaling Emma with what Beth was sure were deeply censored accounts of his life in the Birmingham Royal Ballet, before his retreat to the loot. Dougie, as fair as Tom was dark, was sleek enough to suggest he had to wage a constant battle with his weight. He was in a quiet but expansive mood, talking to Beth with enormous contentment about their new home.

'It's all done, now, every last room. And the garden – Beth, darling, you must see our garden. All hollyhocks and delphiniums and foxgloves. A real cottage garden. All it needs is a maiden in a mob cap to make it look like one of those jigsaws we used to do as kids. Well, that's the plan at least. Whether the slugs and snails will have mercy on us, goodness knows. They had every last one of our hostas!'

'There are always slugs and snails in hostas,' Beth said.

Dougie leaned forward. 'And what slug has got into your hosta, sweetheart? It's no good your pretending that everything in your garden is lovely, you know. You've lost – what – a good half-stone. You're pale. Your hair – well, I just hope that this is simply a bad-hair day. You've lost your bloom, sweetheart. Like that poor, lovelorn Anne Elliot. You know, in that novel.'

Beth nodded. '*Persuasion*. But it's not love that's draining me . . .'

'Oh, no?' he twinkled.

She sighed. 'Just work.'

Dougie's hands and eyebrows shot skywards, returning under gravity in a gesture of resigned irritation. 'I told you. Didn't I? Didn't I say it was no job for you? All those revolting children and no sixth form to leaven the lump?'

'Dougie, it can't be given to all of us to teach in one of the country's best direct grant schools.'

'Sheathe your weapon. I'm out of it now, remember. And every time I switch on Radio Four or open my newspaper, I shed another tear of compassion for you. And all those like you. Tossed round in the good ship *Education* by the rudest of politicians' winds. Dear me, that sounds terribly vulgar.'

'Don't tell me: you meant to imply simply hot air—'

'And it sounded more like farts!'

Emma must have caught the last word and glanced over, eyes wide with a shock Beth would have sworn was genuine. These poor kids – however sophisticated they wanted to be, there was always an Achilles heel, wasn't there? Her own mind made an eccentric rush to a pig called Falstaff, so far rejected as too unclean for Emma. And to a house too old and dark. What would it be like, Conrad's house?

'Hello! Are you still there?' Dougie fluttered his fingers in front of her eyes. 'I said, what do you propose to do about it?'

'I'll have to make an appointment for an interview with one of my careers staff, won't I? "Now, shall I stick this out or quit now and go and run a brothel in Nice?" "Oh, I don't know, Dr Holyoake. Depends if the Nice appointment maintains your pension entitlement."'

'I hate to ask, but what on earth brought the idea of becoming a madam into your mind?'

The arrival of the waitress with their aperitifs spared her having to reply. And, all in all, she was rather relieved. What on earth had her subconscious thrown up?

'I ought,' Dougie said, 'to apologise for Tom. Sometimes he does get it into his head to flirt, you know.' He nodded in the direction of Emma and the young man, strolling down the main street ahead of them and stopping from time to time to peer into touristy shops. 'What if he breaks her heart?' Tom was whispering in Emma's ear.

'Emma's heart is supposed to be safe in the hands of another young man,' Beth said. 'Not, come to think of it, quite as young as Tom. Or – though he's very good-looking – quite as beautiful.'

'Isn't he just? Oh, Beth, it still makes my heart stand still just to watch him walk. So young, so beautiful, so stinking rich – and yet he's chosen me!'

He looked near to tears. Beth slipped her hand into his and squeezed it.

He retained her hand. 'But what on earth are we going to do for you?'

'I may not need anything doing for me. You see, I do,' she said mock-coyly, 'have a gentleman admirer. A follower. Someone who wants to walk out with me.'

'Well, bless my soul! Three of them.'

'Just the one. One Christopher Starling.'

'Well, it could be worse. Just. He could be a sparrow.'

'Another friend says he – Christopher, that is – would rather be a Red Kite. Or a Golden Eagle.'

'I can quite see why. Tell me about this Starling. Does he strut about your lawn in bright plumage digging for leatherjackets?'

'Leatherjackets?'

'Oh, grubs, Beth, nasty little grubs that grow into unlovely insects.'

'Don't talk like that about my pupils! Oh, Dougie, do I have to marry him to escape them?'

'Is it the pupils? I wouldn't have thought there were many kids you can't lick into shape. Oh, that's nice. That dress. You'd look lovely in that.' He pointed into a shop window.

'I would, wouldn't I?' She slowed to a stop and peered. 'It looks as if it's my size, too.'

'Put a note through the door and ask them to put it by for you . . .'

'Till next Christmas?'

'Don't be silly. It'll only take you half an hour – well, forty minutes – to get here after school. In that sexy little car of yours. Oh, dear; what have I said?'

Beth let Tom and Emma draw away even further before she explained.

'Conrad Tate! *The* Conrad Tate? God, I was in love with him for years! Weren't you? God, Beth, you were.'

'No, I wasn't. I had that crush on the pianist – whatshisname . . .'

'So you did. Conrad Tate. Well, there's your answer. Get him to pay for it. Now what have I said? For God's sake, Beth, the man's supposed to be as rich as Croesus!'

'But he didn't smash my car up. Emma did. And Emma earns whatever shop assistants earn. And I can't get hold of her parents to discuss everything with them.'

While she explained, Dougie took her by the arm, making her face him. 'I don't know what's going on in your life, Beth, but there's too much of it. Why don't you come and stay with us for a couple of days? The moment Emma's out of your hair. Come and be cherished.'

Cherished! How long was it since she'd been cherished? To her horror, the kindness in his voice brought tears flooding to her eyes. 'Don't be sorry for me,' she said, turning furiously away. 'I've got what I always wanted: an excellent job, for all you think it's a mere comp; a huge salary; a sexy car; my own home. I'm completely independent.'

'You may be independent of other people,' Dougie observed, leaning against the shop-front and folding his arms, 'but I'd say a lot are still dependent on you. And in any case, to have what you've always wanted may mean you wanted the wrong thing in the first place.'

'Your *best friend*? But he's a man!' Emma turned round in

124

the passenger seat to stare at Beth, too astounded to fasten her seat belt.

'He can say anything to me and I can say anything to him. That sounds like best friends to me. We always take each other as we find each other – we don't have to make any effort to pretend. I'm just as fond of him in his gardening clothes as I am when he dresses up to take me to Glyndebourne. The opera,' she added.

Emma pulled a face. 'But we all put on nice clothes today – yes, you said to.'

'Because I know it gives him pleasure to see his friends well turned out.'

'You mean like Tom?'

'Tom and me. And now you – he likes you very much.' Well, he would: Emma's manners couldn't have been better. Maybe one day she'd grow up to be a lovely butterfly.

Emma might not have heard. 'Tom's great, isn't he? I mean, just . . . just wicked!'

Oh, dear; was using what Beth thought of as kiddie-lingo a bad sign? 'He's certainly a very good-looking young man. Now, are you going to phone Conrad and ask if it's convenient for us to pop in and see him?'

'Oh, he won't mind. He said he was only going to do some work.'

'Well, you know how people are: some don't like being interrupted . . .'

'Like you, you mean.'

Beth couldn't detect any malice. She gave a wry smile. 'Like me.'

'Bored? I can't be bored! I've got a ton of work to do, Emma and Beth just a phone call away and I'm talking to my favourite pig. No, I can't possibly be bored.'

Falstaff grunted.

'OK. Not bored. Bloody frustrated. I only have to think about Emma to want her. I sit at the computer and want her.

125

I play my guitar and want her. I talk to you and want her –
see what I mean?'

Falstaff grunted.

'I suppose I could always go for a walk. All those people
out on the moors. All those Volvos full of children and
dogs. Now that's what we could do, Falstaff. We could get
a harness for you and I could take you for walks. You'd fit in
the back of the Range Rover, wouldn't you? And it'd give
you a change of scene. How about it?'

'Well, why didn't you leave a message, then?' Beth asked,
putting the key into the ignition. 'He could have phoned
back and I could have turned back or gone another way.'
She tried to sound sweetly reasonable, but knew she was
failing. She had wanted so much to see Conrad's farm. And
his house. Not to mention Falstaff the pig. Conrad had been
so disappointed, so hurt, at Emma's reaction, hadn't he?
Well, he wouldn't be disappointed by hers. Anyone putting
all that time and energy – OK, and all that money – into
rescuing so old a house deserved praise and encouragement.
And praise and encouragement were her stock in trade. The
other thing, of course, was that it would have kept her away
from her paperwork for another couple of hours.

'Oh, I hate those things. They always make you say the
wrong thing and you can't change it. I suppose we could
still go.'

'Not a lot of point if he's not there. Or maybe he's left the
machine on because he's working and doesn't want to be
disturbed. OK, let's head for home.' She put the car into gear
and pulled away. Whether it was the car or the prospect of
uninterrupted work for the rest of the day, she felt thoroughly
miserable.

It was only when she surfaced for a nightcap at eleven that
she realised Emma wasn't in the house. She'd heard her shout
up something about going to get a video – what time would
that have been? Oh, God. Now what?

Come on, Beth: Dawlish is hardly an inner-city slum, and

126

after life in Coventry Emma's going to be streetwise. Sure there's a sea wall to fall off and sea to drown in. But she wouldn't be going anywhere near the sea wall anyway. Emma's not one to take a longer route anywhere than absolutely necessary. She's got her mobile phone: it's as good as grafted on to her. And that might be the answer: Conrad must have phoned her, and she's gone off with him, not to get a video. But she said something about a video.

She gripped the sink, peering through the window at the narrow road outside. Hopeless, of course. She'd only see if she switched off the light.

Switch off the light, then.

Look, Emma's eighteen. Imagine how she'd feel to come in knowing her aunt had been checking on her movements from behind twitching curtains. Remember how Mum used to check up on you but never on Russell. Give the girl some space.

Making herself breathe deeply, Beth allowed herself another finger of whisky.

And if she isn't in by eleven-thirty, ring her on her mobile.

There was nothing to come between Beth and a full night's sleep: Emma had come in while Beth was cleaning her teeth, and had gone straight to her bedroom; all her paperwork was ready for the following day; she had a reliable car to get her to work.

So why didn't sleep come? Why was her pulse thumping away as if she'd run up the hill? Hell, why couldn't she just switch off her brain as she'd switched off her computer. She'd saved all the data, gone through the close-down procedure – and was still awake. Lying there wasn't doing any good. She'd better get up and do something. Even if it did mean going back up to her study. She could put the fire on, have another drink, and sift through the Sunday paper she hadn't even opened yet. The trouble was, she wanted talk, kind human talk, the sort Dougie had offered today. Or maybe sex with Christopher. No. Just talk. The sort she'd had with Conrad last night, come to think of it. What if – just suppose what would happen if she phoned any of the three men. Well, she couldn't phone Dougie and disturb him and Tom. No, that was out. But the other men would be on their own. Would Christopher tell her to come straight over? Would Conrad?

Whatever else he was doing, Richard had always—

No. No, no, no. She must not go down that road.

Nor, she thought sourly, the way of the whisky bottle. She reached down a book at random, opening it where it would.

To be loved to madness was her great desire.

She closed it again, quickly. What she'd better do was get a duster and clean some of the shelves.

Why not go down there, right now? Conrad looked across the town to where he knew Emma would be sleeping in Beth's bungalow. Impossible to pick it out, of course, in the dark. But there was nothing to stop him simply slipping the car into gear and heading down there. He could tap quietly on the window. *Rapunzel, Rapunzel, let down your long hair!* She'd love the romance of it. And he was sure she wanted him to make love to her as much as he wanted to. Why not? He'd make sure they didn't wake Beth.

Then a light came on. And another – yes, in Beth's study. My God, it must be her lights he'd seen last time he'd gone for a nocturnal drive. Poor woman. If she suffered from insomnia, no wonder she was looking so washed-out. No chance of the sort of oversleep he allowed himself. What a bright pair they were, prowling round when every sensible soul was deep asleep. He snorted. If he drove down, it shouldn't be to rouse Emma, but to soothe poor Beth. He had a sudden vision of the two of them, wrapped round each other on her sofa bed, two sleepless babes in the wood. Where on earth had that thought come from?

The light went out.

Seventeen

It took Beth more effort than she liked to stride into Jane's office, but she wasn't going to be seen shuffling with fatigue anywhere in her school.

Jane hardly raised her head. 'You know there isn't a single slot in your diary for the next three days?'

Oh, God – what did that announcement herald? Beth rested her case on Jane's desk and waited.

'Well, we're going to have to make one. That policeman's here again. About the fires.'

'That policeman?' Who on earth was she talking about?

'Yes.' Was Jane really blushing? Surely not! 'You know, the detective.'

Rather than look a complete fool, Beth nodded. 'The nice one,' she said, as encouragingly as if she could remember him.

Yes, Jane was blushing. 'Well, he was polite, I suppose. And . . . quite attractive. Anyway, he wants to talk to you again. What shall I cancel to fit him in?'

'Can you give me the diary? Then we can go through it together.' Beth gathered up the case – she really should make time to work with weights again – and let herself into her office. 'And – sorry, Jane – I'd die for a coffee.'

Though she laid the diary on her own desk and opened it, she didn't look at the day's page. Or at anything except space. This was what she'd lain awake all night worrying about, and now she had to confront it. Arson. Someone had started a series of fires which had culminated in the loss of their paper supply. The attacks had now stopped, as abruptly

129

as they had started. Her brain could no more have failed to do the right sums than it could have failed to add an extra factor she hoped the police hadn't got to yet. Who stood to benefit from the fire? A panicky GCSE candidate? Some miserable child who simply wanted to get out of a test? An habitual troublemaker? Or someone with much more to gain?

Jane was already bringing in her coffee. 'Though if you ask me you should cut down on your caffeine. Look at you. You're not going to tell me you slept last night. Again. Is it that niece of yours?'

'Partly. She was late coming home and I was worried—'

'She's eighteen, isn't she? Well, then.'

'Even so . . .' It wouldn't help to prophesy that Jane would have the same anxieties over Tessa in a very few years. 'OK, whom can we least afford to offend and whom can we delegate to?'

Jane pulled a face. 'No one and no one. When are you going to get yourself a deputy? You can't keep on dumping on subject heads and heads of year.'

Beth laughed: 'Whose side are you on? Come on: we can bring in Head of Pastoral Care. Look: two interviews with parents. He can do those.'

They shuffled and negotiated for the next five minutes.

Beth rubbed her face. Why did sleep want to seize her at such a silly time when it had been so elusive all night? 'OK. I could see this policeman about ten. What did you say his name was?'

'Keane.'

'I'm sorry?'

'David Keane. He's a detective inspector. About forty. Fair hair.'

'Will he be bringing a sidekick, like on TV?'

'There's a DC Kemble. A woman.' Jane oozed disapproval.

Beth had been right about that blush. 'Kemble and Keane: how very theatrical,' she said lightly. Equally lightly, she hoped, but doubting it, she added, 'Now, before you get on to the phone, would you be kind enough to get me the minutes of the governors' meetings for the year before I arrived?'

Jane stared, as well she might.

'I just fancy a little light reading,' Beth lied.

Her heart was heavier than she could have imagined when Jane showed in DI Keane – yes, of course she remembered him now! – but she gave him what she realised was her usual headmistressy smile. The one she favoured Emma with all too often. She must remember to ration its use to work.

David Keane responded with what she suspected was an equally professional smile. Presumably the sort that had made Jane blush had been altogether more relaxed – one that reached the cool grey eyes, for preference. His handshake was fine – a good, firm grip. And Beth supposed he was attractive enough when he wasn't bristling at something. What was making him go stiff-legged as a terrier she couldn't guess. Perhaps he was an insomniac too.

They smiled some more, and sat, she alongside, not behind her desk. That should help establish a more relaxed atmosphere. Friendly co-operation – that was what was needed. A tap on the door announced Jane and a tray of tea things – the start of her campaign against Beth's caffeine intake, no doubt. Or perhaps because she'd already established that Keane didn't like coffee.

Waiting till they were alone again, Beth said cautiously, 'How are your inquiries going, David? Pointing at any of my reprobates?' They'd got on first-name terms straight away last week – more as a result, she suspected, of police policy than of any particular liking. But he was a man who brought a blush to Jane's cheek, so she must try to be friendly.

He took a biscuit – Jane had produced the sort usually reserved for Starling! – but laid it in his saucer. No, a neat body like that wouldn't consume many calories. 'I'm not convinced. Those that were in school were where they were supposed to be, according to the registers and their teachers.'

'Even Dean Simmons?'

Keane's smile shifted an inch further up his nose. 'An impeccable alibi: in an interview room at his local nick discussing an accusation of shoplifting.'

'The skivers?'

'Most of them were where they said they were; I must say, Beth, you've got a remarkably low absenteeism rate.'

'We've just had an Ofsted inspection: however much you loathe inspections, they don't half make you tighten your ship. If that's possible. Though it sounds as if I've killed a metaphor somewhere.'

When he laughed, his whole face lit up. Jane's blushes got more understandable by the minute. 'You aren't like my old headmistress.'

'I hope,' she said tartly, 'I'm not like anyone's old headmistress. God, there were some horrors around. Mind you, there are times when I have to be a horror. Like you with a rookie constable, perhaps. After all, we both work for hierarchical organisations based on very firm discipline.'

He sipped his tea: presumably he wasn't interested in a philosophical discussion, and who could blame him. All she was doing was filling in time till she could decently ask whom he suspected – or at least, where his investigations would next take him. She'd waste no more time. 'So if one of the kids didn't do it, who did?'

'Staff? Someone you've had to discipline?'

'Jane must have given you copies of their timetables – but I'd bet most of them were where they were supposed to be, too. Not many free periods for teachers in the twenty-first century.'

He nodded, ticking something in the notebook he'd produced. 'Any other suggestions, Beth?'

She took a deep breath. 'The only thoroughly disaffected member of the team isn't in fact a teacher.'

'You're talking Jeff Bromwich here?'

She blinked. 'Am I? Oh, of course I am. But I'm not alleging anything. The point is, he'd have access to the whole building – even the out-of-bounds parts. Though I'm sure you've already worked that out.'

His nod was grim. 'His alibi seems OK, though. Any other possibilities? Any vengeful ex-pupils – kids with a grudge?'

'You had the list of those last week too. I'm sure you've checked every last one. In any case, the security cameras would have picked them up, wouldn't they? You do have the video footage? What's the problem?' For clearly there was one.

'How many people would know that your budget doesn't stretch to keeping film in them all?'

'You're joking!'

'That's what Bromwich says. He says you cut the budget at a meeting not so long ago. What I'd like to know, Beth, is why.' This time there was no trace of a smile.

'What I'd like to know is where he got that idea from. Machete raids, problem parents, arson, the deranged – all schools have to prioritise security. Government policy. Backed, incidentally, with funding. Even in somewhere like Exeter.' She watched him write.

'You'd deny refusing him permission to renew worn out tapes?' His face was suddenly transformed. 'I must say, your secretary says you'd be more likely to have stomped off and bought him one.'

'Or even more likely, I'm afraid, to have sent Jane stomping off to get one. You've already spoken to her about this,' she added, trying not to let anger flare.

'She raised it with me when I asked for copies of memos you might have sent about security. She struck me as the sort of woman to keep memos.'

Could that be a criticism of Jane? 'She is simply a perfect secretary. A super cook. A lovely woman.' Hell, did that sound too much like a testimonial?

'So why should he allege you told him otherwise?'

'Because he's an idle toad.' She had to say it. 'In a case like this, don't you usually ask who'd most benefit?'

'In arson we often ask who'd get most twisted pleasure. Why did you ask that? Did you have someone in mind? Come on, Beth, if you suspect anyone, you must tell me.'

'I have nothing at all to base any suspicion on. But if I do find anything, I promise I'll tell you immediately.'

Keane sat very tall. 'Let me tell you this. It's not your job to go hunting for evidence. If you have any reason to suspect anyone, it's more than your job, it's your duty to tell me.' His face softened minutely. 'In absolute confidence, of course. No?' He stood. So did she. No one was going to try to tower intimidatingly over her. 'There's such a thing as perverting the course of justice, you know.'

'There's such a thing as wasting police time, David. Come on, you can't investigate someone just because my bunion twitches. And you have my word that if the other bunion even thinks about twitching, I'll phone you.'

His grey eyes locked on her blue ones. He jabbed the air three inches from her chest. 'You phone me.'

Good cop, bad cop all in one. He did them both well, too. Beth sat down, reaching for the Governors' Meetings file. She had to read through that before she allowed herself even to think the thought that was pressing against her brain. But not now. Here were the senior staff who'd be on the following day's interview panel for the Art post. A little something to take home, then. She slipped it into her already overloaded case.

So how could she get hold of Tom's phone number? Emma realised with a thud to the stomach that she didn't even know his other name. Just Tom, a ballet dancer. Well, an ex-ballet dancer. With a rich aunt and a weak ankle. And the most gorgeous profile she'd ever seen. And lovely strong-looking hands. And she didn't even know his name. Shit and shit and shit!

What about the other one? Beth's friend. The one with fair hair. What had she called him? Some silly name, not a real man's name at all. She sat up in bed, scratching her scalp. She'd better wash her hair this morning.

Her head still swathed in a towel, and wearing just her dressing gown, Emma picked up her toast and wandered through into Beth's bedroom. Where would she keep her address book? No, none of the dressing-table drawers – they were full of underwear. Now, who'd have thought Beth would run to sexy suspender belts? The wardrobe – no shelves or anywhere for an address book. Bookshelves – just books. Of course! Slapping herself on the head with irritation, she headed up the stairs to Beth's office.

God, what sort of woman locked filing cabinets in her own house? Talk about secretive. What about the computer? You even needed a password to get into that! Picking up the toast she had one last bite: it was cold and leathery. She dropped it in the waste-paper bin and went downstairs for some more. It was only when she was in the kitchen she thought that the compost bin might be a more tactful place to leave it, so she trailed back up again. She even shut the door behind her. And the bedroom door.

She was just buttering the next piece when she thought about the phone in the living room. She might look there. She took the toast through with her, laying it on the table top. Not even a phone book. Never mind. She might as well see what was on TV while she was here. And then, just about lunchtime, she might stroll down to the shops. Gaz said he often had a half of scrumpy at lunchtime. She'd timed the visit to the video shop nicely last night – he'd been ready to cash up. So they'd had a nice drink and some chips together. Perhaps things wouldn't be so bad when Conrad went. But she must remind Beth about that doctor's appointment.

'Sweetheart! Whatever is the matter?' Conrad took one look at Emma and gathered her up. Only when he'd soothed her tears did he hold her away from him, and then only long enough to mop them. 'My poor sweet. What is it?'

'I want to go with you, Conrad. When you go to this

conference. It's Auntie Beth. She's really started to get her
knife into me and I can't bear it. Soon as she gets in she
starts on me.'

'Where is she?'

Emma pointed. 'Up there.'

Well, he just hoped Beth's study was soundproofed. She
wouldn't want the neighbours to hear what he was going to
say. But even as he worked himself up into a rage, he had
doubts. A week ago he'd have believed anything of her.
Now he wondered if there'd been some crossed wires. But
however crossed they'd been, Beth had no right to upset a
sick girl like that. None.

There was no reply when he tapped at the door so he
went in. 'Beth? What the hell—' He bit off his question.
You couldn't shout at a woman as pale as that. Her face
was almost grey. 'What's up?'

'Nothing.' She was fingering some papers on her desk.

'When two of you are awash with tears, I'd guess something's the matter.'

'Two of us? Oh – oh, God! I didn't mean to upset her.'
She put her elbows on the desk top and dropped her face
into her hands.

'Well you have. Good and proper. What's it all about?'

She shrugged. 'She'd been through my things. And then
denied it.'

'So why did you say she had?'

'Because she left toast crumbs on my desk, on my filing
cabinet, on my dressing table and in my silk underwear.
OK? I just asked her not to.'

He had to steel himself. 'You must have done more than
just ask her.'

'Conrad, I couldn't do more than just ask anyone anything
this evening. I'm bloody shattered.'

She looked it. But she straightened herself up. 'Look –
could you tell her I'm sorry if I upset her.'

He nodded but sat down. 'What was she looking for?'

'God knows. The first time I thought it might be tampons

or something. But not this time. You don't keep tampons in a filing cabinet.'

'Have you tried asking her?'

She looked him in the eye. 'I was afraid if I did I might lose my temper.'

He had an impulse to comfort her almost as strong as his desire to hold Emma. Something had gone wrong, and he'd never know what it was – probably neither of them would either. Emma was upset. But so was Beth. And it sounded as if she might have right on her side. But a woman like her didn't sit and weep just because of a tiff with a girl.

'You want some aspirins?'

'Three, please. Soluble. Bathroom cabinet.'

Accepting an offer like that wasn't Beth's style, he reflected, watching the tablets fizz. She must feel bad.

She was still at her desk when he came back. He put the glass into her hand, but she barely registered it.

'Look, Beth. The best thing I can do is take Emma out of here for a bit. I'll come up when she's gone to bed. If you'll still be up, that is? Go on, drink up.'

She drank the aspirin mixture, shuddering. 'Still be up? The way things are, Conrad, I shall be lucky to get to bed tonight.'

Eighteen

If Conrad wasn't careful this would turn into a first-class row, the last thing he wanted, especially in this tiny restaurant, where every word could be overheard.

Emma wanted to go to the States with him. She had a passport, didn't she? They could easily get it from Coventry, and she had to go to Coventry anyway to get her sick note extended and they could do both on the way to the airport and why was he being so unkind?

'I just can't take you. Not this time. It's work, Emma. You'd be bored out of your skull,' he explained for the umpteenth time. 'When I get back, if you still want to go, I'll take you. I'll take you anywhere in the world. I promise.'

'You can book last-minute flights on the Internet. And in the States they book rooms, don't they, in hotels. Not beds.' With her lip stuck out like that she looked about twelve.

Conrad worried a fingernail. There'd be room for half a dozen Emmas in the accommodation into which he'd been booked. And there was another point: it would separate her from Beth, who certainly needed a respite.

'It's not a matter of flights or beds, sweetheart,' he said, trying to sound patient and loving, not irritated. 'It's work. I shall be busy round the clock. It's only for a week. Less than a week. I'll take you back to Coventry by all means—'

'I don't want to go to bloody Coventry. I want to go with you.'

'I know. And I'd love you to come. But just for this

particular week it isn't possible. I shall phone you every day – I've promised that.'

'Well, I shan't be there when you do. Anyway, who'll look after me in Coventry?'

'Your parents. We must get in touch with your parents somehow. In any case, you're nearly better now, Em. You're looking after yourself at Beth's, aren't you?'

'But there's stuff in her freezer and she does the shopping. And you take me out. Like now. How will I manage?'

From somewhere he heard an echo of Beth's dry offer to give him a cook-book.

'I'll buy you a whole pile of ready meals,' he said, gently, desperate not to laugh. 'All you'll have to do is microwave them.'

Should he give in? Should he take her? But the whole point of this masquerade had been to make sure she loved him, not Conrad Tate, ageing superstar. The last thing he wanted to do was drop her into the middle of a very tightly scheduled rehearsal period, including, of course, attendant media hype. If the media got to her, they'd make mincemeat of her – she hadn't an ounce of the guile needed for dealing with double-edged questions. Sure, some of the group's wives and girlfriends would gather round to protect and advise her, but he had a feeling she wasn't a woman's woman and might not take kindly to their company. Or their advice.

Emma burst into tears. He passed her a couple of the handkerchiefs Marie took such pride in ironing. Should he learn to do it himself or should he rely on paper tissues? 'Come on, sweetheart; we're supposed to be enjoying ourselves while we can. Pop into the ladies' and make yourself beautiful for me. Please. Pretty please.'

She pushed away from the table, grabbed her bag, and flounced off.

The wine waiter approached to top up his glass with mineral water.

'You wouldn't fancy some of our house wine, sir? We

do it by the glass. And you might fancy something to calm you down after that lot.'

Writhing at his disloyalty, knowing he ought to snub the man, Conrad nodded. 'Red for me. And a glass for the young lady, too. Sweet white.'

He watched his hands as he waited: the trembling was subsiding.

'There you go, sir. These daughters know how to give their old dads a hard time, don't they?'

'They do indeed.' Conrad hoped his smile wasn't too tight. Was that what they looked like, father and daughter? Well, who the hell cared what it looked like! No, he mustn't glower. He must smile his welcome to Emma, as and when she took it into her head to grace him with her presence. And then he'd got to be charming to her for the rest of the evening. He could imagine the look on Beth's face when he told her all about it. It'd be great, wouldn't it, just to slip away now and retreat to that wonderful study. Good conversation, good whisky or good wine. A real refuge.

He looked at his watch. Ten minutes, now. The wretched child had got him, hadn't she, by the short and curlies. He couldn't go and get her; couldn't even ask a waitress to go and get her, in case she came back with a horribly public message. Well, he must just sit it out.

Somehow he must make the evening sound funny, so he could watch the pain in Beth's face easing. Maybe he should give her another massage. Yes, that would be good. He smiled at the thought of her back and shoulders responding to his hands, loved the memory of her little moans as he touched the tight spots. There'd be enough of them tonight. What on earth had happened to reduce her to the state she'd been in earlier? It couldn't just be Emma's looking for whatever it was. Which ought to be his next question when Emma deigned to reappear: what had she been doing? But he had an idea that that was a question best not asked, not yet.

Fancy the two women looking so alike – OK, apart from the eyes, Beth's blue where Emma's were that wonderful brown; and Beth's extra couple of inches in height; and being so different in personality. There was still time for Emma to develop, of course, to grow some of the steel which made Beth into such a successful woman. Steel! Poor woman, it must be rusting now. What could he do to make her really happy? Flowers? Perfume?

Bugger all, lest Emma resent it.

Fifteen minutes. He caught the waiter looking at him speculatively. How dare the stupid girl expose him to this? But even as the anger rose, he had a terrible fantasy that she might have slipped out of another door. What then? They were deep in Haldon Moor, for goodness' sake – she couldn't skip on a bus home from here. What if . . . ? No, his car-keys were safe in his pocket.

Jesus, what if she tried to walk? At the very least she'd get lost; at the worst – no, he couldn't contemplate the worst. Couldn't contemplate the thought of her being picked up by some sick rapist.

What the hell should he do?

The wine waiter was back. 'With my daughter,' he said, 'I find the best thing to do is send a message saying her soup's going cold. Shall I ask one of my young lady colleagues to do the necessary?'

The bastard! The absolute bastard! Sitting there, eating his supper as if he didn't give a shit about her. He smiled and passed her the serviette – sorry, Mum, napkin – as if she'd just been touching up her lipstick. The trouble was, she needed him to get away from here. No bloody buses, no bloody taxis. And if he thought she was going to leg it home wearing shoes like this he was mistaken.

If he thought she was going to apologise, he was bloody well mistaken. No, she wouldn't even speak till he'd apologised to her.

And the soup was horrible.

Beth was looking a little better, no doubt about that, sitting on the sofa in the living room. But she was still terribly pale, and he was almost glad that Emma had stomped off to bed – still without speaking.

'Have you eaten?' he asked, as quietly as he could. The last thing he needed was for Emma to decide to erupt with a complaint that if he wouldn't speak to her, he shouldn't speak to anyone. Especially Beth, of course.

'Home-made soup. Emma fancied some the other day and there was a lot left over.'

Little minx, putting poor Beth to extra work. And then leaving it as she'd left the soup tonight.

'You'll have to give me the recipe,' he said. He told her what Marie had said. Most, but not all, of what Marie had said. 'So long as it's easy.'

'Very easy,' she said. 'And it does taste very good so long as you make sure the vegetables are fresh.'

'No problem with Tucker's Hay – organic, straight from the kitchen garden.' He smiled. 'Where do you keep your red wine? Isn't it supposed to have medicinal properties? Soothing the troubled breast?'

She laughed. 'That's music. As for wine, St Paul recommends it for your stomach's sake. Maybe he knew about it controlling cholesterol. Anyway, it's in that big cupboard in the kitchen.' She pulled herself up.

'Stay where you are. Hang on! What was that?'

'The front door. Emma. Going out.'

He was ready to give chase. But stopped. 'Am I supposed to run after her and grovel?'

'Very much so. Aren't you going to?'

'Not until I've got us our wine. And then, maybe, very slowly. I've had a bit of an evening with her.'

'Tell me,' she said. Just as he'd hoped she would.

She was just making up the sofa bed when she thought of it. 'Your car!'

He clapped his hand over his mouth. 'Shit. She finds that here and she'll – God knows what she'll do.'

'She'll look for you in her bedroom,' Beth said carefully. How much of that wine had she sunk? 'And when she doesn't find you there, she'll look in the living room. And when she doesn't find you there . . .'

'She'll come pounding into your bedroom looking for me there. Shit!'

'Conrad – far be it for a woman in my position to advise anyone to break the law. But for Christ's sake go and move it. Round the corner. She won't notice it there.' She crossed her fingers.

He responded by crossing his eyes.

How easy, how very easy, to laugh with him.

She made up the bed in his absence, too weary, no, too drunk to explore all the implications of what they were doing. Conspiring against her niece, his lover. Conspiring with each other. After a wonderful, silly hour, in which they'd talked about everything except important things. God, what a lovely man. Completely wasted on Emma, of course, who would lead him a merry dance and leave him, taking as much palimony as she could get her paws on. What a mess Russell and Sylvia had made of their daughter. Except that it didn't always work like that. The best parents, goodness knew, had disastrous kids.

'Penny for them.'

He was back, stowing his keys in his pocket.

'I was just wondering . . .' No, she couldn't say it to him. She couldn't tell him she was wondering how Emma would turn out, eventually. '. . . how late she'd be,' she concluded.

His smile said he knew she was lying, but he leaned across to ruffle her hair. 'Look at the height of you,' he said suddenly. He'd been drinking too, of course. 'It'd be lovely dancing with a woman as tall as you.'

'Even lovelier for me, dancing with a man I didn't look down on.'

There was a pause, as if he was making some sort of decision.

They could dance up here, couldn't they? They could move the furniture, push back the rugs and dance on her wooden floor. Music? He looked – yes, she'd got little loudspeakers either side of her computer. But he couldn't be bothered with bloody computers now. How often did she get to listen? He'd never heard music in this place. Never. Yet downstairs she'd got a whole drawer-system full of CDs – all sorts of stuff. Yes, all his early stuff. And his contemporaries'. And a lot of serious stuff – looked as if she had a passion for Mozart. Imagine dancing to Mozart. Imagine dancing to anything in this lovely light warm room, imagine dousing the lights and dancing in the light of the moon and stars shining through the windows in the roof.

He held out his hand, as formally as if he were at a ball. Equally formally, she took it, and laid her other hand on his shoulder. For music, he sang, almost under his breath. All the big dance classics. All the big love songs. There they were, two figures pale in the moonlight, turning slowly, slowly, as if they had all the time in the world. Round and round they circled. For the first few moments she'd been tense, as if embarrassed. Then she relaxed into his pace, letting him lead, moulding her steps, her body to his. He lost all sense of time and place. Looking at her closed eyes, he knew she had too.

The front door snapped shut. Emma was home.

Beth froze. As gently as he could, he laid a finger to her lips, shaking his head. But he didn't let go of her. Nor did she try to move away.

That was Emma running water to clean her teeth. That was Emma flushing the loo. That was Emma closing her bedroom door with a smack loud enough to have woken Beth had she been downstairs. He felt Beth flinch under his hands. Before he could say or do anything, she stepped gently but firmly away from him.

'She hasn't noticed my car, then,' he said, trying to sound amused. 'But I'll have to be up early to move it.'

'Do you want me to give you a call when I leave?'

Her voice was too light, as if she was trying to control it.

'Good idea.' His was, too. No doubt about it.

'I'll go and lay out the breakfast things – call me when you've finished with the bathroom.'

'Very quietly!'

They nodded at each other. She led the way downstairs.

Hell, he had to go to the loo! All that wine! Hell and hell and hell. Beth had probably just dropped off to sleep, and that was the worst time to be woken. Stupid sod – why hadn't he thought of a bucket or something?

It was no good, he'd have to go. Padding barefoot as quietly as he could, he opened the door little by little. Trust Beth to keep it well oiled. OK, down the stairs, grateful that she was a woman who left her curtains undrawn, grateful that there was moonlight.

Any obstacles? Shoes? Clothes? He paused on the bottom step to check. No, she'd tidied everything.

He smiled affectionately at her. Yes, she was a good woman. My God, a beautiful woman, too, sleep easing the frown she'd worn too much these last few days. The loose hair, the curves of her face – he wanted to touch the silvered outlines. Wanted to touch her lips, take the weight of her breasts, feel those long, strong legs around his waist.

For Christ's sake, Conrad, the bloody loo!

He'd no idea how long he waited for his blood to stop pounding, for his desire to subside. No idea. He felt sick: Emma was sleeping just feet away and he wanted her aunt. Oh, God, he wanted Beth, more deeply, more desperately than he'd imagined it was possible to want a woman, and now he had to walk past her, not waking her, and steal back up the stairs, silent as a thief.

And then he had, quietly and finally, to shut the door on her.

Nineteen

Beth was awake long before the radio alarm came to life with the sounds of argument on the *Today* programme. She forced a rueful smile: with all the arguments in her life, perhaps she'd be better off with a bell. No, too many of those at school.

It was no use lying here hot-eyed. She must get up in absolute silence, so she didn't wake him. It would be best, wouldn't it, if she could slip straight out without even bothering with breakfast. She had to forget about it, put it right out of her mind. So they'd danced. OK. She'd danced with Emma's boyfriend, that was all; it was Christopher she had a date with tonight. Everything would be fine, if she could only sweep it all under the carpet.

Fine.

No. Not fine at all. There were some things that couldn't be ignored. Sooner or later she had to face Conrad. Talk with him about what had happened. But not yet. Not till she'd damped down the fire he'd started.

She looked longingly up the stairs. What if she went up and took him? Took him as he drowsed, pulled him into her? Yes!

No.

Cold shower time. And pray God it worked.

But even the sounds of a cold shower woke Conrad, and he was there, sleep-ruffled and unshaven, in the kitchen when she came out of her bedroom.

Had he been lying awake too? Wanting her as much as she'd wanted him?

Nonsense. He had a girlfriend. Emma. Her niece.

For whatever reason, he was quiet to the point of awkwardness. And he avoided eye contact. Was he angry with her for last night? Or angry with himself?

'I really haven't got time . . .' she began. With the hire car she had plenty of time.

'I'd really like,' he said, through a mouthful of toast, 'to talk to you. Since it's my last day. I could run you in to work.'

'I'd like that . . .'

'But you've got the sodding Fiesta, haven't you?'

'No reason it can't stay on my drive.' She mustn't sound as desperate as she felt.

He produced a savage smile. 'Better make sure you take the bloody keys with you.' He swallowed, as if the toast were suddenly dry. 'Is it today yours is supposed to be ready?'

'Should be. But I make a point of not believing promises made by garages – even if they do belong to your friends. In any case, it might be better to take a taxi home.'

'Oh, yes. You're having a meal with that Sparrow bloke, aren't you?'

'The Red Kite,' she said, wishing that her smile didn't hurt.

'Quite.'

'If you're sure about taking me . . . ?'

'Quite sure. Just give me two minutes.' He ran his hand over his chin. 'Then I'll come and help Emma pack and take her back to Coventry. Out of your hair.' For a moment she thought he was going to reach out and touch it. But his hand dropped. He bit his lip. 'Then I'll go straight off to the States. That's best.'

They were in his car before she said, 'I know you're angry with her. But you'll soon forget and forgive. And as she gets better she'll be less . . .'

'Like a naughty kid?'

What if he couldn't forgive Emma? What if he came to love . . . No, she mustn't even let the thought take form.

He said nothing, a couple of jaywalking pheasants giving him the excuse.

'What if she tries to stow away?' She spoke as lightly as she could. What she wanted to tell him was to plug his ears, like the ancient sailors avoiding – my God, she'd forgotten who. He'd know. But there were other more important things to say if only she could find the words. She stared at him dumbly.

'I can't let her. Don't you see, I can't let her. What the fuck's going on?' He braked to a vicious halt at the end of a ten-car tailback.

She blinked. She'd never heard him swear before. 'Just someone broken down.' But as it became their turn to pass the hapless motorist, she said, 'Conrad, it's my secretary. We're going to have to stop and help.'

As she got out of the car she heard him muttering a string of obscenities under his breath, and she found herself echoing them. Why, why on earth, on this morning when she'd wanted him just to herself, did they have to stop for someone else? And, something heavy in her stomach told her, give Jane a lift all the way to work. With Jane's sharp eyes; watching them, there'd be no chance for any but the most perfunctory farewells. No, she could say a warm goodbye as a friend. That would be all right.

But it wasn't what she wanted.

There, everything was as tidy as he could make it. He wanted her home to be nice when she came back to it, so she'd know who'd done it and think of him. Even more, he liked touching things she'd touched. He enjoyed sitting in the chair she sat in to use the phone, sensing a faint breath of her perfume when he picked up the receiver. Yes, everything was tied up: no problems with Tucker's Hay or with the New York ticket. At least they'd kissed when they'd said goodbye. Had she been as determined to kiss him as he her? That bloody secretary, taking it all in. But she'd definitely reached for him and hugged him – he closed his eyes, desperate to recapture the feel of her body against his. And she'd kissed him, cheek, cheek, then lips. He found himself smiling. No, it wouldn't be an easy day, but at least he knew what he had to do.

At last, he checked his watch. Time to get moving. Time to wake Emma and tell her to get her things ready. He might as well do it kindly. He took a cup of tea with him as he knocked on her door.

Beth had been there on the other side of the table often enough to empathise with the poor candidates. They were in the middle of the group session at the moment, gathered round the coffee pot, making frantic attempts at civilised conversation. Any moment now they'd have their tour of the building and in half an hour they'd make their individual presentations and submit themselves to a grilling. In her younger days, Art teachers had almost prided themselves on their eccentric dress. These were all city-slicker clones, desperate to impress and pick up what would be quite a lucrative post.

Conrad would be wearing jeans and sweater, wouldn't he. Almost his uniform. Camouflage, more like. But how anyone as attractive as he could become so invisible, she'd no idea.

And yet he had, hadn't he! Not just at that concert but on Dartmoor, when Emma had had to be rescued from the horses! My God! How could she have been so blind? And how come he'd never mentioned it? He must have recognised the car. When he came home tonight . . . But he wouldn't be coming home, not tonight, maybe no other nights.

But headmistresses interviewing for jobs didn't clap their hands to their mouths and run weeping from the room. They didn't so much as bite their lips, not even the lips Conrad had kissed an hour before. They smiled at the earnest young candidates and asked kindly, 'Now, has anyone shown you where the loos are?'

149

$$* \quad * \quad *$$

Conrad stood in Beth's kitchen his head in his hands. No. It wasn't true. It couldn't be true. But it was. And somehow he'd got to break the news to Beth.

The interview panel had just smiled the first candidate out of the room and were jotting down their responses when Jane tapped at the door, putting her head round without waiting for a response. She caught Beth's eye and mimed a phone.

'Urgent,' she whispered. 'Very urgent, or I wouldn't bother you, Dr Holyoake.'

Beth was on her feet. Of course it must be urgent, for such a session to be interrupted. She gestured an apology at her startled colleagues and found her dignified stride becoming a scuttle.

Jane almost ran to keep up with her.

'It's that friend of yours. The one that gave me the lift. Said it was a matter of life or death.'

Despite herself, Beth grinned. Conrad would know he'd have to say that, wouldn't he? All the same, she shut herself into the office to take the call, and braced herself, scarcely breathing.

Where the hell was she? Why didn't she come? Should he ring off and try again? No, that'd lose him the line, and God knew it had taken him long enough to get through. He'd have to tell her about that, that her switchboard wasn't up to the demands made on it.

'Conrad?'

'Shit, Beth – I don't know how to tell you. It's Emma. She's ill again. Really bad. I've sent for the doctor. I wanted . . . God, I've got that plane to catch and I need . . . Beth, we have to talk.' He was stuttering and stumbling like a teenager. 'Beth . . . it's you . . . Shit, there's the front door bell. I have to talk to you. Shit!' He had to go to the door, didn't he? 'Just hang on. Please.'

He opened the door to a kindly-looking man, well into his sixties. Emma'd be all right with him. And he had to talk to Beth.

'You're still there? Beth, I have to tell you. Sod, he's left the door open. I'll phone you from London, right? And from the States? And – Beth, don't believe anything the media say, anything at all, right? Promise!'

'Promise. Conrad, what's—'

'He's coming out now. Beth. Sweetheart, I have to go. I'll call you. Soon as I can. I . . .'

The doctor looked at him oddly. As well he might. Conrad pushed open the nearest door. They stood in the kitchen.

'Just a return of the glandular fever, Mr . . . er ?'

'Tate.'

The doctor had clocked him, hadn't he? Shit.

'Nothing to worry about. Often happens. Bed rest for a couple of days. She'll be fine.' He picked up his bag, but hesitated. There was more, wasn't there?

Conrad waited.

Nothing. The doctor scribbled and dropped a piece of paper on the table. 'She says she needs a sick note. That should cover her until she can get back to her own doctor. Is there anyone to look after her?'

Conrad looked at his watch. 'I fly from Heathrow in eight hours. And her aunt works full-time and a half. And as for her parents – God alone knows where they are.'

'Perhaps,' said the doctor dryly, 'it's time to have a word with Him. In the meantime, ask Beth to call me, will you?'

Three more candidates to go. Until the last question had been asked, the last reply given, Beth had to keep her mind off what it kept circling back to. Better even to think about the sick Emma than about Conrad. Mustn't think about Conrad. Must think about removal expenses and local schools for the children of the woman in front of her. Must wonder why the candidate was asking as many questions as the panel.

Must remember to raise that with the panel afterwards. Sweetheart. He'd called her sweetheart. He probably called all his women friends sweetheart.

'Thank you, Ms Gordon,' she said, smiling to encourage her. 'Now, as we've told all the other candidates . . .'

All the bastard had done was leave the aspirin within reach. And the water. It'd serve him right if she took the lot. Leaving her like this. The bastard. Cold and icy as Beth, he'd accused her of bringing it on herself. Tantrums, he'd called them. And he'd picked on her for staying out late last night. Well, that was his fault. And she'd told him so. And then she'd cried, and asked him to stay.

He'd shaken his head, very serious, just like Beth or Dad. 'Emma, you know I can't stay. I have a job to do. And it seems to me a little rest from each other wouldn't be a bad thing. We've both got some thinking to do.'

It was the way he'd said *both* that had worried her. He couldn't mean it! He couldn't mean that he didn't love her any more. Couldn't.

It wasn't fair, him leaving her like this. Wasn't fair.

He must have another woman. Yes, that was it. Some woman in the States. That was why he didn't want her to go. He was two-timing her. Bastard, bastard, bastard! She threw the empty glass at the door he'd closed two hours ago and gave herself up to tears. The dreadful thing was, she'd told Gaz not to come here. So he wouldn't even know she was ill. Then she found a smile. Perhaps he'd come anyway.

'The trouble is,' Beth said, 'there's no clear-cut winner. Or loser. So it seems to me we may be in for a long meeting, ladies and gentlemen. Would you prefer me to arrange to have our lunch brought in to us, or would a few hunger pangs serve to concentrate our minds?'

'Which would you prefer, Elizabeth?' Starling asked, an edge of sarcasm to his voice.

'I think the latter is kinder to our candidates, if not to us.

152

Now, what I suggest' – Hell! She should be leaving this to Christopher, as Chair of Governors! – 'is that I hand over to Mr Starling and the process can begin.'

They exchanged gracious smiles.

Nightmare scenario! Each panel member backed a different candidate. Some at considerable length. This could go on for ever, and it wasn't the food Beth wanted but the phone.

It was no good, was it? He wouldn't use the phone while he was moving, and couldn't stop to use it. And the chances were that Beth would still be in-sodding-communicado. Well, she had a job to do, same as he had. And if he didn't pay more attention to the road – where had that bloody container lorry come from? – he wouldn't be doing it. Death at this stage definitely wasn't on the agenda.

'Any more phone calls, Jane?' Beth asked, too weary to feign indifference.

'I'll give you the list when you've had a coffee. I'll bring it through to you. That was a marathon session, wasn't it?' she called, through Beth's open door. 'I didn't think it looked too good when you suddenly asked for lunch to be sent through. Here.'

Beth managed a smile. 'A marathon,' she agreed. It would be such a relief to pour it all on to someone else's shoulders, but though she knew in her bones Jane would say nothing to anyone, she couldn't breach confidentiality even that far. It wasn't fair to Jane, anyway. It was the Head who was paid to carry such problems, not the Head's secretary.

'You look as though you could do with a shot of something in that,' Jane said, turning to close the door firmly behind her.

'No way. I've got to cram in my day's work before I – oh, my God, I was supposed to be having supper with Starling, wasn't I?' She clapped a hand to the side of her face.

'"Supposed"?'

'My niece – that phone call, the life-and-death one, was about Emma. She's had a bad relapse. I've got to go back and look after her.'

'Are you sure it's a good thing to stand him up at this stage?'

'I can't not. If the girl's ill—'

'He won't like it, you know.'

He wouldn't like the way Beth had argued against him for her preferred candidate. Not, as it happened, the gay one. His gender-orientation hadn't entered into it, as far as she was concerned. He was just a truculent young man. But she'd fought, in the end, for the first candidate, an African-Caribbean woman. Starling had thrown his weight behind a soccer-playing Scotsman. It wouldn't help their future relationship that when the panel had finally split evenly, Starling had used his vote as Chair to clinch his choice. He'd done it with every appearance of charm and grace, true, but he'd done it.

'Likes his power, Mr Starling,' Jane added. 'The first batch of paper's arrived, by the way. Very prompt, wasn't it?'

'Very,' Beth echoed dully.

'Look,' Jane said slowly, 'you helped me out today in a big way. It's Tessa's week with her dad. Why don't I come and babysit your niece for you? I'll even run you home so you can introduce us.'

Beth flung her hands in the air. 'She's eighteen. She'd probably resent it like hell. She probably doesn't *need* anyone there at all, but I can't not be, if you see what I mean. Family and all that . . . Oh, Jane, bless you but no.'

'So what do you tell Starling?'

'The truth. He won't like it, but if he's a decent man, he'll understand, same as you understand. Funny, anyone else I could suggest a take-away on our knees in front of the telly.' Anyone else she could dance with barefoot on her study floor. No. Not with anyone. With Conrad. 'In fact,' she said slowly, 'maybe that's what I should do. Offer it as a substitute. See what he thinks.'

Taking the empty mug, Jane patted her shoulder. 'If you want a lift home, the offer's still there. I know the lad from the garage; he's bringing the car round by four thirty. Which is more than your garage will be doing, by the way. They need at least another twenty-four hours, they said. And here's the rest of the phone messages.' She moved a list in front of Beth, and then shifted the phone slightly. 'Oh, and you'd better put Mr Starling at the top, hadn't you?'

Beth shook her head. 'If you're serious about that lift, I'll phone him from home. In fact, I can do most of these from home, so you won't have to wait here till pig's squealing time.'

'Till when?'

Beth stared. 'I wonder where I picked that up? Somewhere on my educational travels!' Well, if she couldn't have Conrad to talk to, wouldn't it be wonderful to have a pig called Falstaff as a confidant?

Twenty

'**M**y poor, dear Elizabeth.' Christopher's voice came kind and soothing over the phone. 'Of course I understand. No – not one word more. There's no need to apologise. I'll simply transfer our booking till – shall we hope Emma will be well enough to leave on her own by Friday?'

She'd never warmed to him so much. He'd made no mention of their protracted struggle earlier in the day, and had expressed nothing but concern, both for Emma and for herself.

'Friday would be delightful, Christopher. Or even Saturday.' She was never at her best after six on Fridays. G and T, a face pack and an early night were her idea of a Friday-night treat. Not that she got them very often.

This time he hesitated. 'That's not convenient. Friday would be better.' He was so decided she was glad she hadn't mentioned face packs or any other frivolity.

Should she offer the take-away option for tonight? Even as she thought about it there was a small moan from Emma's room. No, life was complicated enough without Christopher's presence. Tonight she needed to slip off her shoes, put her feet on the sofa and eat comfort food. Not the sort of thing she could ever imagine doing with Christopher. A TV meal with him would involve you clamping your knees under a polite little table, his knees tight under his. And she had an idea that linen napkins would be involved somewhere. None of the elbows-on-kitchen-table meals she'd enjoyed with Conrad. No. Mustn't think about

Conrad. That way madness lay. Hell! Why had he cornered the market in quotations?

Why on earth had Beth come home so early? She never came home before seven, even seven thirty, and here she was, well before six. And Gaz didn't get home till half-six, he said, at the earliest, and there was no point trying to leave a message with his mum because she could hardly read and write – not that she believed that, but he'd been quite firm about not phoning earlier. Stroppy, really. So how could she get rid of Beth for a bit? After all, even though it was her own mobile phone, and she was quite entitled to use it, she wasn't sure how Beth would react. She'd probably say the sort of thing her mother would say: 'If you're well enough to use the phone, you're well enough to get up and make your own cups of tea.'

Soup. How about asking her to make some more soup? She was sure there weren't any vegetables in the rack. But it would be just like Beth to have a load ready-made in the freezer – yes, some of the soup she'd asked for last time she'd wanted a bit of peace and quiet.

And, come to think of it, she wasn't very hungry anyway. Just tired. Picking up all that glass had really knackered her. She could have left it to Beth, but then she'd have had to explain, and there were things she didn't want to say to Beth about Conrad. Not yet, anyway.

Maybe, when she woke up, she'd like some milk pudding. Or custard. Or something that would send Beth off to the supermarket but not put her to enough trouble to make her ratty.

'Dr Holyoake? Beth? It's Bill Davis, here.'

Bill Davis – once her solid, old-fashioned GP, now retired but doing occasional locum work at the busy surgery down the hill. So he was the anonymous doctor whom she'd been supposed to phone. 'Bill! I was waiting for surgery to end before I called you.'

'We seem to have had a sudden outbreak of good health here, now the word's out that the handsome Dr Wentworth is away. So I've shut up shop early. How does your niece seem?'

'Subdued. But I wouldn't think she's feverish now, if she was before.'

'I thought I'd look in.'

'I wouldn't have thought she was that ill.'

'I was thinking less of the niece than of the aunt. And I know I can rely on the quality of your wine cellar.'

'I'll put something in the fridge straight away.'

So much for a quiet evening in front of the TV. Not that she'd ever have spent one, except in her dreams. More to the point was that an evening's work was down the tubes. But she owed Bill. He'd been exceptionally kind and supportive over the Richard business, not just as her medic but also as a pillar of a community that could have gossiped. Luckily he was a kitchen-table man: the wine would accompany the fish and chips he always brought with him.

She put her head round Emma's door. Was that glass on the floor? Saying nothing, she bent and scooped several slivers, holding them on her open palm until she could wrap them and stow them safely in the bin.

'Dropped a glass,' Emma said.

From the spread of the splinters, it had been a considerably more energetic fall than a mere drop. But teenagers were entitled to tantrums, so Beth just nodded.

'I just came to see how you were, Emma. And to tell you that Dr Davis is on the way – so you might be better popping on a nightie.'

Emma was ready to protest, but she stifled whatever she was going to say.

'Any news of Conrad?' Beth asked. What on earth had made her risk that? Better soldier on. 'Did he get to Heathrow safely?'

'Oh, yes. Fine.' Emma turned from her, hunching her shoulder.

Which meant he hadn't phoned! Was he all right? Had there been some sort of accident? No. She must just accept that he hadn't phoned. That was all.

'Don't forget that nightie,' she said, and withdrew to the kitchen. She must have been more careless than she'd thought: when she closed the bin lid on the glass, beads of blood rolled across her palm.

If he'd had any doubts about quitting, the contrast between his reception on the way to the VIP lounge and the one for some teenie-band he'd never heard of would have resolved them. Conrad Tate, past tense. Boys 'R' Us, or whatever they called themselves, were *now*. Fine by him. He could make his phone call in peace.

Although it was only six, the school phone rang on and on, until a message clicked in telling him that the office would open at eight the next day. At least she'd had the sense to leave at a decent hour. But where would she have gone? To pick up her car? Home? Or straight out with that nasty little bugger Christopher Starling? Her mobile was switched off, but he left a message. 'I'll talk to you as soon as I can. Don't forget that promise. Right?' If she had to listen to that in front of anyone else, at least it wouldn't embarrass her. In any case, what would Dad say if he left a message telling her he was a fool and he'd loved her and not Emma for . . . for how long? When had he realised? Only when it had dawned on him that, while Emma was like all the other pretty little girls he'd always fancied and been fancied by, Beth was something else. A quality woman. A gorgeous, sexy quality woman. Unwithered by age. He had a very good idea that custom wouldn't stale her infinite variety, either. Why on earth had he ever fancied he loved Emma? Ah, something to raise with Sholto the Shrink when he got back.

Her home number was engaged. Before he could even register the call-back system, a voice called his name and he was surrounded by the media who'd abandoned the kids.

Perhaps – judging by their questions about his next album – he wasn't such a has-been after all.

But he wished, as boarding was announced, that he was. He still hadn't phoned her. OK. He could do it from the States. But on impulse he slipped into the loo, pressing redial. Still engaged. He jabbed in her mobile number. To hell with everything. 'I love you,' he said.

'What I want to know,' Bill said, closing the kitchen door firmly behind him, 'is why you're giving house-room to your niece. Who is, as you observed, much better.'

'Because she's been ill and needed a refuge and because her father wasn't well.'

He leaned towards her. 'My dear girl, you're neither green nor cabbage-looking.'

'All right. I was conned. I was happy to have her for a few days, but the few days have stretched.'

'And your car, of course, was crushed.' He accepted the wine and sniffed. 'Now this is one I don't know. It's very promising, though.' He reached for the bottle, holding it at arm's length to read the label. 'Casa Nueva? Chilean! I suppose it's politically acceptable these days?'

'I hope so. This one's so good I'd hate to have to give it up. How did you know about my car?'

'Because some drunken young slob reorganised my wing for me and my car was in the same recovery ward as yours. Which, of course, is instantly recognisable. So I asked Gordon how it had sustained its injuries, and heard about this gorgeous sexy bird who'd smashed it under the wheel arch of his mate's car. Further enquiries elicited the information that said sexy bird was your niece. Your insurance people aren't going to love you, Beth.'

She tipped the fish on to the plates she'd had warming and divided the chips. Three sorts of vinegar and some lemon juice jostled the salt and pepper.

'Well? Gordon tells me it's not an insurance job. You're settling the bill yourself, he says.' He fished out and put on his half-moon glasses. 'Old age,' he said, parenthetically.

'Until Emma's father repays me, yes.'

'Indulge an old man, Beth. Can you afford it? Because if you can't, an annuity of mine has—'

She held up a hand. 'Bill, you're a sweetie. But I'd be embarrassed to tell you what I'm earning; the government thinks we're a Good Thing.'

'And so you are. But people always spend up to their maximum, in my experience. So if you ever need any ready cash . . .' He looked at her over his glasses.

'Thanks. I'll tell you what I do need. Advice on how to pick up and dispose of my various vehicles tomorrow. No matter how I try to work it out in my mind, I always end up with two or none.'

While they ate, they worked out a system of following each other and giving lifts which, though complicated, meant neither would be stranded and both would end up minus hired car and plus their own. The only problem was the amount of time it took from her working day. Well, technically she could take the time, whereas Bill certainly couldn't miss evening surgery. And she'd got to make time to collect cash from the bank, since Gordon had shuddered at the thought of a credit card.

'You're supposed to be eating your supper, not sitting there scowling at it,' Bill observed.

She gave a contrite smile. 'Taking time off always makes me scowl. At least, the thought of the knock-on effects does.'

'So, to return to my original question: why are you adding to an already overburdened life? Why didn't you get that young man to cancel his plans and look after her?'

She pushed away her plate. So Conrad had given the impression that he and Emma were still together. Perhaps they were. Perhaps Emma hadn't been lying.

'His plans were set in tablets of stone.' Would Conrad have recognised the allusion? 'Mine . . . will still bend a

bit. And her parents will be home soon. I'm not sure,' she
added carefully, 'that they'd have liked the idea of their ewe
lamb being looked after by a young man.'

'Ewe lamb! My dear Beth, the reason I came tonight
– *one* of the reasons: you know what I mean! – was
to observe to you, in the most non-judgemental way I
could, that your Emma is knocking around with – indeed
practically fornicating with – the same drunken young slob
that reorganised the wing of my car. The same drunken slob
who's fathered at least three kids in this parish over the last
two years and is currently beating his common-law wife so
badly that I'm in hopes of getting her to press charges.'

'Emma's on the pill,' she said faintly. How could she
have taken up with someone else – someone like that! –
so soon after Conrad? No, while Conrad was still . . .

'Oh, Beth, pregnancy's the least of your sexual worries,
these days! Surely you know that! He's into drugs as well
as drink—'

'In Dawlish!'

'You don't think the twentieth century – sorry, twenty-
first century! – has entirely passed us by? We're within
spitting distance of Bristol or Plymouth – drugs for the
asking, there. That young man is danger, Beth. And young
Emma – how much has she got between her ears? How
streetwise is she?'

'I wouldn't have thought Coventry was a hotbed of
innocence. Bill, what the hell do I do? Without breaking
your confidence? Without making it look as if I'm sending
her home because I can't be bothered with her?'

'You lie. Tell her I've recommended she goes to her own
GP for tests – I can tell you some mumbo-jumbo, and I'll
write to him and explain. And don't send her, take her.'

'How the hell can I do that? If I have to go through
hoops just to pick up a car, how on earth can I take her
to Coventry – and, of course, stay there with her? If one of
my staff asked me for time off for that sort of reason I'd
bloody kill them.'

'And?'

'And probably give them the time off. But I can't, I truly can't, take the whole week off to look after someone else's child.'

'What happened to your milk of human kindness, Beth? I have to tell you, I expected better of you than this.'

His tone, his words, hurt. She stared at him, her eyes filling with tears. Before she knew, she was sobbing, whether with anger or misery she didn't know. All she knew was that before she could dive from the room a pair of elderly arms had encircled her and she had found that rarest of things, a shoulder to cry on.

Jesus! Beth was only snogging the doctor. He was supposed to be checking on her, not sitting feeding his face and swilling wine with Beth. Wasn't there something about professional conduct or something that meant doctors weren't supposed to do it with their patients? Now, which was best, to go back to bed and let them get on with it? Or burst in on them and catch them at it?

Shit! He must have seen the door move.

'Come in, young lady,' he said. 'Or rather, go and put on that pretty dressing gown of yours and then come in. You mustn't risk getting cold, you know. That could have very serious consequences. An infection of any sort could have very serious consequences.'

Jesus! What had he meant by that? She got the dressing gown, and tied it up as far as she could. As an afterthought, she dug out the slippers her mother had made her pack and popped those on too.

He was sitting in the kitchen waiting for her, leaning forward on the kitchen table – what had happened to all the plates and everything? – just as if he was in his surgery. She sat down opposite, carefully hitching the dressing gown closer. He peered over those awful glasses. As for Beth, she had her back to them both, fiddling with the kettle. Trying to pretend nothing had happened, no doubt.

'Now, Emma, you don't need me to tell you how unpleasant glandular fever is. And you know there's no cure.' He sounded very serious.

'My doctor gave me antibiotics,' she said. 'For my throat.'

'Well, there's no throat infection now, as far as I can see. But that doesn't mean you won't get another one.' He lifted a finger as if to stop her speaking. But she wouldn't have interrupted, not him. 'Now, you may have heard that in the old days glandular fever was known as the kissing disease. When it's in its incubation stage, it seems to pass from one young person to another very quickly – and it was assumed that it was when they kissed. The thing is, Emma, passing germs can be a two-way thing. It's not just you passing your germs on. When you get close to anyone, when you kiss someone, they can pass theirs to you. And I don't need to tell you that you simply must not – in your weakened state – take that risk. Am I making myself clear?'

My God, what was she going to get? Emma nodded.

'Now, the safest place for any patient is her own environment. I'm extremely anxious to get you away from here, because Beth, working with young people as she does, is highly likely to bring back here – bring back to you, Emma – all sorts of undesirable infections. Should anyone have consulted me about bringing you down here at all, I would have advised absolutely against it.'

She swallowed. Was her throat hurting again? My God, if Beth had brought any bugs back! 'But my doctor—'

'Almost certainly didn't know that your aunt worked at a school. Now, Emma, you need to be looked after somewhere much safer. I understand your parents are away, however.'

They'd come back, though, wouldn't they? 'Would it be safe here for another day? Until they came?'

He stared at her. 'I should think so. Provided you stayed in the bungalow and had as little contact with your aunt as possible.'

'Her! She's hardly ever here!' She'd gone into the conservatory: perhaps this nice old guy had told her to keep
clear.

'Thank goodness for that. Now, how do we get hold of
your mother and father?'

'I'd better phone. Hey, is it OK to use the same phone
as Beth uses?'

He fished in his bag. 'I think you should use these sterile
wipes. Now, off you go, young lady, and the moment you've
phoned, back to bed with you. Or I can't answer for the
consequences.'

Twenty-One

B eth waited in the conservatory, her shoulders still shaking, but now with laughter. As Bill appeared, she turned and held out her hands to him.

'That was worth an Oscar. Oh, Bill, you're my hero!'

'It's a good job I'm a doctor as well. God, woman, you're as stressed as they come. I think we'd better wait till that little madam takes herself off to bed and then you can pour me a glass of your excellent whisky and tell me everything that is, as Emma would say, bugging you. And, if I might make so bold, you could while away some of the time giving these poor chaps a drop of water. You'll lose them if you don't.'

'Hang on; did I hear the phone?'

It would be too late for Conrad, wouldn't it? No point in rushing. She could just let the answerphone take it. If Bill said the geraniums should be watered, watered they must be.

'Bill,' she began, five minutes later, up in the relative privacy of her study, 'what I have to talk about is so confidential – this sounds paranoid, doesn't it? – that I'm going to put some music on the computer while we talk.'

'Don't make it too loud: I've lost some of the frequencies,' he said, touching his left ear. 'And I really do hate Mahler. And I shall shut you up if you try to talk against Mozart.'

'How are you on – let me see? C. P. E. Bach?'

'Fine. Now sit down and tell me.'

She swallowed. She tried again, shaking her head.

'You're pregnant?'

No wonder Emma had been putty in his hands if he'd looked at her under his eyebrows like that.

'No. A chance, as they say, would be a fine thing. And don't worry; I'd be round to the clinic before you can say "ovulation" should the need become remotely likely.' What if she'd tried to seduce Conrad this morning? What a fool even to have thought of it! She must make an appointment fast.

'So the rumours about you and a handsome man aren't true?'

Her head flew up. 'Rumours? Me and Conrad?' Then she realised how stupid she must sound, and the blush spread from her stomach to the roots of her hair and beyond.

Though he couldn't have failed to notice, he merely said, 'That wasn't the name I heard. Though you can talk to me about Conrad if you want. I fancy that must be the man who called the surgery this morning.'

What was he holding back? It was safest just to nod.

'So who else might you want to talk to me about?'

'Whom did you hear rumours about?' she parried.

'Ah, you're feeling better. You always were too nifty for your own good at verbal tennis. The man with whom your name has been linked is Christopher Starling, widower, of Topsham. A very eligible man, Beth – no doubt about that.'

'Extremely.' She counted on her fingers. 'Handsome – well, good-looking in a rather fleshy way. Kind. Generous. A good citizen. A very hands-on Chair of Governors.'

'On the committee of his golf club. A respected employer. A regular church-goer. Sounds just the man for you, Beth.'

'You wouldn't be a member at this golf club of his, would you?'

His eyes narrowed to match hers. 'Why would you want to know that?'

Beth's shrug was extravagant. 'Male bonding? Locker-room gossip?'

'Ah. You're checking him out before you commit yourself. Well, since his wife died he's not led a monastic existence, but you wouldn't expect that.'

'Any particular relationships? Like one with my predecessor?'

He looked at her sharply. 'You're not about to go all missish?'

'No. He can have slept with half the women in Exeter for all I care, but I want to know about his relationship with – what was her name? Caroline Sands?'

'Caroline Sands, indeed. A charming and intelligent woman – though not in the same league as yourself for either. Nor – and please don't be offended by this – as hard-headed. I'd have said she was much more . . . pliable. She never had the fights you've had with the governors.'

'She sold half the playing fields to pay for the new Languages Block.'

'She did. Or rather, of course, the governors did. To a builder.'

'Whose ticky-tacky houses I long to hurl a hockey ball through every time I drive past them. Do you know if the builder has any connection with any of the governors?'

He looked shocked. 'Come now, the Education Ministry or whatever it's called these days wouldn't have let that go through. Everything must have been above board.'

'How long did she and Starling go out together? And when did they break up and how and why?'

'Their business, surely.'

'Oh, absolutely.' She couldn't keep the irony out of her voice.

'You don't think it is?'

'I do. If it's a simple matter of two people. But she did something some people might find reprehensible during her tenure . . .'

'Hundreds of playing fields have been sold in the last few years. That's why the English can no longer play cricket or soccer.'

If she wasn't careful she'd get side-tracked. 'Now, someone's asked me to do something pretty reprehensible.'

'To sell the rest of the grounds?'

'No. On the contrary. Someone's asked me to buy something. And I did something . . . dishonourable . . . to help them sell it me cheap.' She explained.

'If as a governor he's entitled to see the tenders, I don't see that you've done anything wrong. Even if you don't think it was right.'

'But don't you see – he's actually benefited from the fire. And no one else has any motive at all.'

'Arsonists don't necessarily need motives.'

'That's what the police said. But you see, I started to think about who gained most from the playing field sale. And I wondered what – if anything – he could have got out of it.'

'You've lost me. Let me try and catch up. He enjoys a friendship with your predecessor who sells the playing fields. The relationship ends. He begins a relationship with you.'

'But only very recently. Very recently indeed. And – maybe I'm being hypersensitive – but his initial ardour seems to be cooling very quickly.'

'As well it might if he suspects you're keen on another man.'

'I'd have thought that he was the sort of man who would see that as an absolute challenge. So I'd like to know at what point his previous relationship ended and why. You see, I've got this tiny lurking feeling . . .'

He waited but must have gathered she'd go no further. 'He enjoys a friendship with you who buy paper. You're now suspecting him of arson and of corrupt dealings over the playing-field sale. It's a bit tenuous for me, my dear. Perhaps if I had a drop more whisky I'd think more clearly. And before you ask, I know that will put me well over the limit, but it's a fine night and I shall enjoy the walk home. The last fine night,' he observed, peering round the blind at the sea, 'for some time, if the forecasters are to be believed. Our American friends are despatching an extremely deep depression across the Atlantic. I heard the gale warning to shipping tonight. I always pray,' he added, unexpectedly, 'for those in peril on the sea.'

And, God, for those who fly across it. She gave Bill a generous three fingers' worth.

'How would I find out, Bill, if Starling could have benefited from the sale?'

'If he's as clever as you seem to imply, only with great difficulty. It seems a very odd thing to me, Beth, to want to prove something like that against a man who, as far as I know, only has the most honourable intentions towards you.'

'I don't want to prove it. I want to disprove it. Get it out of my mind. Come on, there must be some gossip. It's not as if the clubhouse is the confessional. Who are his contacts?'

He was looking older, tired. 'If I tell you, what will you do? I don't want you getting involved in any amateur detective heroics.'

'You have my word,' she said seriously, pouring another finger of whisky. 'Here. Have as much as you like, Bill, only promise me one thing: you'll take a taxi home, preferably Dan Cobley's.'

'That old gossip's? Why?'

'Because I want it all over Dawlish by six tomorrow that you did not spend the night here. I strongly suspect the presence of Conrad's Range Rover hasn't gone unnoticed. I'm sure everyone thought he was Emma's boyfriend until . . . until . . .'

'Her activities with the unlovely Gaz. Well, I'll accept that condition, provided you meet one of mine. This Conrad – tell me all about him.'

'All I can,' she agreed, crossing her fingers behind her back.

He listened in silence. At last, covering the glass with his hand when she offered more, he said, 'So he's an eligible young man, good-looking and with a home on Dartmoor. Very nice. I suppose you don't know he's a pop star too? One of those all-boozing, all-drug-abusing, all-womanising pop stars? Come on, Beth; you're not telling me that you've fallen for a pretty face.'

'You recognised him,' she said flatly. 'You didn't say

anything to Emma, did you? You see, he was courting her as an ordinary man – didn't want her to fall for his image.'

'How very touching. And you, my dear – have you fallen for him as an ordinary man? Or as – what do they call them? – a megastar? And how are you going to tell your niece – who may be a damned nuisance but may be credited with some feelings, perhaps – that you're after her young man?'

'Her ex-young man,' Beth said, surprising herself with her firmness. 'Anyone who two-times him with the loathsome Gaz doesn't deserve Conrad.'

'And you weren't two-timing the worthy Starling with him? Oh, come, Beth; indulge an old man. You're sure about this Conrad, aren't you? That he's a decent man. But how does he feel? I'd hate you to get hurt.'

But this was the question she couldn't answer. She parried with another. 'So who are Starling's buddies? Would any of them have benefited by the playing-field sale?'

He raised his eyes heavenwards. 'He plays occasionally with a builder. As I do. But you wouldn't be thinking I slipped him a few prescriptions so he'd build the surgery extension cheap?'

'Might he have built anything cheap?'

Bill looked very tired. 'Apart from those acres of houses? Well, I understand Starling opened a new factory recently – you know, making that dreadful furniture. And I've an idea I know who might have built it.'

'You realise that this is a very serious allegation, Dr Holyoake.' David Keane's sudden formality emphasised it if nothing else did. It was as if it was he on the power side of her desk.

'It's not an allegation, Inspector.' She paid back in the same coin. 'It's a rumour. You asked me to contact you if I had the merest breath of suspicion . . .'

'I thought it had something to do with your bunions twitching.' His face softened.

'One started to twitch. I called you. I've told you. What

more can I do?' She pushed her hair back and started to worry an earlobe. Richard would have recognised the signs immediately. No. Mustn't think about Richard. Time to pull herself together. 'I must remind you you've guaranteed complete confidentiality in this. I absolutely do not want to be involved.'

'If what you . . . you *suspect* . . . is true, you'll have to be involved sooner or later.'

'Later. Not sooner. I'm happy to go to court. But I don't want to be a . . . grass. You've used your bunion, not mine, David. You'll phone my predecessor about her dealings with Starling on your instinct, not mine.'

He smiled. 'Detectives are allowed to have instincts only if they're backed with evidence. If there's evidence to find, I'll find it. If not, I'll control my instincts and cosset my bunions.'

'I'll be the first to buy you comfortable slippers. Now,' she asked, 'can I offer you tea or coffee? I told Jane not to bring any in while we were talking, but by this time in the morning I should be on my third caffeine fix.'

He looked at her seriously. 'Tea's better. Better still one of those herbal teas. Much better for you in the long run.'

What had been best for her so far was one of Bill Davis's magic pills. It had knocked her out as soon as she'd taken it, already lying, as ordered, in bed. All the tumble of anxieties about Conrad had been stilled. Until morning, at least. The best plan, she decided, was to keep them at least suppressed by dint of hard work and action; hence David Keane's arrival soon after nine. Till then she'd been so busy tackling what she should have done the previous day and had so signally failed to catch up with at home that she'd almost managed. Hell, the few sentences Bill had got out of her had sounded so pathetically like the outpourings of a teenager even younger than Emma that they must both have been glad when she shut up. She certainly had been. The trouble was that the pain of hearing his voice aloud was balanced exactly by exquisite pleasure.

He hadn't phoned. Whoever had phoned last night hadn't left a message on the machine. Or had they? Even as she held the yellow pen to highlight the latest of the Secretary of State's diktats she saw in her mind's eye the light flashing on the machine as she'd walked into the house. Had Emma really listened to all the messages and then wiped them? No. She wasn't capable of such malice. If it was malice. Why did she keep jumping the gun like this? What if she'd simply answered the phone and pressed the wrong button? Wasn't that more likely, given Emma's general lack of technological know-how? The dreadful thing was, she didn't think she could face asking her. Because the even more dreadful fact was that she didn't think she could any longer believe a word Emma said. To think, all along she'd known how to reach Russell and Sylvia! Presumably it had suited her to stay in Dawlish because that was where Conrad would find her. And if not Conrad, Gaz. What sort of story had she spun her parents over the car accident? For Beth to introduce the subject – not to mention the matter of payment – would require the same sort of Machiavellian planning that had underpinned Emma's moves.

As it happened, she might have rather longer to do it than she could have wished. The storm-force winds that Bill had forecast the previous evening were already bringing driving rain, and warnings had apparently gone out about surface water on the motorways. High-sided vehicles had been stopped from crossing exposed bridges. This weather meant business. Loving and indeed indulgent father Russell might be, but he'd always been a man who liked his weather fine, and Beth wouldn't be surprised if he preferred to sit out the storms in the comfort of an anonymous hotel room at Gatwick.

Meanwhile, she had a school to run. What she might just do was take one of her regular strolls round. It wouldn't just be pupil problems she was checking this time. It was whether the security cameras had film in them. She'd done weird things in the past. Not too many eyebrows would be raised if she went round carrying a stepladder and a key. Apart from Jeff Bromwich's, of course.

David Keane fiddled with his cuff, as if she didn't know he was checking his watch. She could have told him it was seven minutes past twelve.

'You're sure it couldn't have been some of the kids larking about?' he asked for the fourth time.

Why did he always pretend at the start of conversations to be so hostile? She prickled back. 'Of course it could have been. One could have sat on another's shoulders to reach the camera, there's no doubt about it. But we'd have them on video doing precisely that. But the security company assured me that their system of keys plus a combination code would make it impossible to do more than vandalise the system. The video mechanism and the tape itself would remain inviolate.'

'And the only people to have access to a key and knowledge of the code are yourself and Jeff Bromwich.'

'Yes.'

'You're sure about that?'

Exasperated beyond endurance, she flung her hands in the air. 'David, I know it's your job to press questions like this, but I don't have time for constant reiteration. I have a school to run. And I'm rapidly running out of time to do it.'

'So what on earth made you check in the first place?'

'For God's sake, what do you want me to say this time? An eccentric whim to parade round the premises carrying a lightweight set of steps? A perverted sense of exhibitionism, since I was wearing not trousers but a skirt?' Beth stood up. As far as she was concerned the meeting was over. 'Just get on with your job, Inspector, so that I can get on with mine.'

To her astonishment he grinned. 'If I do, do you reckon Jane will make me a cuppa?'

Why not? 'So long as she makes me one too.'

*   *   *

Emma peered as far down her throat as the bathroom mirror
let her. It looked OK. But then, what were throats supposed
to look like? What if Conrad had given her something those
times he'd kissed her? Poor Conrad. All that time she'd
thought he was being a coward and really he was being
noble. Well, next time she saw him, she'd make sure he
wasn't noble. She'd make sure their tongues worked as hard
as hers and Gaz's the other night. God, what if she'd got
something from *him*? They said spots were a sign of lots of
that hormone, test— test— whatever. And that blokes with
spots were extra sexy. But they said spots were catching too.
Nasty red and yellow zits! Ugh. Ugh and double ugh!

Back to the mirror! No. A bit of a blackhead there, but no
zits. She looked round the bathroom. What if she used some
of Beth's posh cleanser? That should fix them. Where did she
keep that sort of thing? No, nothing in the bathroom cabinet.
It must be in her bedroom along with all her other stuff.

She'd better not take any toast along this time. No point in
getting Beth on her case yet again. Let's see. Cleanser. Pat in,
tissue off. Toner. Which moisturiser? God, she'd got enough
to open a shop, hadn't she? Which smelt the nicest?

It wasn't often Beth gave Jane her orders in the staff loo, but
this was one of them.

'You're free this lunchtime – right? Or this evening. If he
asks you out, you're free.'

'Beth, I—'

'Do you like this man or not? Well, then.'

'Do you really think he will?'

'How do I know? But if he does, remember what the man
in the film said: *Carpe diem!*'

Jane blushed, then asked, 'Does that apply to you as well
as me?'

'Why?'

'Because I meant to tell you: that young man phoned.'

Conrad!

'I told him you were incommunicado,' Jane continued. 'Beth – did I do wrong? Oh, I'm sorry – I'd have put him through if I'd known . . .'

Oh, God. Beth managed a smile. It must be enough that he'd tried. 'Next time,' she managed, 'whatever I'm doing . . .'

'He said – he actually said it was more than a matter of life and death,' Jane said in a rush. 'And you were to remember his promise.'

She had to have a moment alone. 'Go and be nice to David, Jane. Oh, the whole of lunchtime if you can. Go on!'

She leaned on the nearest washbasin, grateful for the cold seeping into her hands. Yes, he must—

'Oh. Miss. Sorry.' A child ducked in and out.

But Beth was faster.

'Gabrielle! Gabrielle Strout! Come back here!'

The child's pell-mell bid for escape faltered.

'That's better. Now, Gabrielle, I believe you're in the top set for English. How is it that someone in the top set for English is unable to read the simple words on that door. What do they say, Gabrielle?'

'Women Staff Only.'

'Women Staff Only what, Gabrielle?'

'Women Staff Only, Dr Holyoake . . .'

God, what a mess! Emma mopped. Well, that was the worst gone. Even so, there was no way Beth wouldn't notice this! And there was no Conrad to take her to Plymouth to buy more. Well, Dad always said the best form of defence was attack. And – if she really mustn't hang out with Gaz – she had the whole day in front of her.

Twenty-Two

'But I want to go home *now*. Not tomorrow. *Now*.'
'Emma, love, they've advised people not to travel.'
The phone made her father's whine sound worse. 'You won't remember that hurricane we had – and there was that one in France not so long ago – but they're saying they're expecting another. You stay in the warm and dry with your Auntie Beth. Your mum and I will be with you as soon as we can.'

'But she's being so horrible to me. And half the time she isn't here anyway. And the doctor said you really shouldn't expose me to all the germs she's bringing back from that gross school of hers. Dad.' Yes! He was hesitating. 'Dad. Please.'

'I'll talk to your mother. And maybe phone the AA. Yes, I could do that.'

'So you'll come? Oh, Dad—'

'No. I didn't say that. I said I'd see. Now you go back to bed, if that's where the doctor said you should be. I'll ring you the minute I can.'

She flung down the phone. God, he was so horrible. Why was everyone so horrible to her? It was so boring. All this stuff about the weather – it was only raining a little bit. She drifted to the window to have a better look.

What was Beth's hire car doing on the drive? How had she got into work? Had that doctor she'd been snogging stayed overnight and driven her in? No. His car was still in the lane opposite. The businessman who fancied her – Starling? No. She hadn't heard his voice. Nor seen the Beamer.

177

Christ!

She was through Beth's bedroom and up the stairs – what if . . . ?

But the room was just like it was last time. All those books, the computer, the filing cabinets. No answers there. Not unless she could find the key to the cabinet. No sign of that. But there was still the rest of the house, wasn't there? Starting with the dishwasher. Which was where she'd found – hadn't she? – the pairs of breakfast things. Yes, same again. Two mugs, two plates. If it wasn't the doc, wasn't Starling, who was it? What if it was Richard again? No. Couldn't be. No, the only bloke it could be was – no, it couldn't be. It must be. Christ, she'd make her sorry. She'd get him back again and rub Beth's stuck-up nose in it. Let Gaz poke her? No, she'd be in bed with Conrad before . . . before she could say 'fallope'.

'It's a good job neither of us wears a wig,' Bill shouted to her as she emerged from Gordon's garage, her bank account now distinctly unwell.

They'd done it: returned his hire car; travelled in her hire car to pick up her MG; trailed back to the Teignmouth hire depot to return hers; next time they'd go back to the garage for his Volvo. And they were still on speaking terms.

'You'll come back for a cuppa to celebrate?' she yelled back. The wind whipped the words from her mouth.

'Why not? Goodness, Beth, imagine being one of those poor beggars out there.' He pointed down the street into the bay, and then, almost as if hypnotised, led her out on to the promenade. The sea itself had been whipped into a brown-grey porridge and, however threatening it might look to those on the shore, was still a refuge to an increasing flotilla of merchant ships. Her eyes streaming as her hair lashed into them, Beth gave up counting at twenty.

'And there'll be more by morning,' Bill added. 'Pray God they all get into shelter.'

'Amen.'

Beth led the way back from Newton Abbot. She'd been disingenuous, to say the least, in inviting Bill back home. Just by being there, however, he'd offer at least a temporary respite from what she was sure would be a verbal storm. Emma, after all, wasn't to know that Bill had been talking eyewash simply to help Beth. If she thought Beth had genuinely put her at risk, she'd whip herself briskly into hysterics.

Whatever she'd been expecting, however, wasn't as bad as she got.

'You bitch, you cow,' Emma began, the moment Beth opened the door. 'You—' She'd clearly been taking language lessons from Gaz.

'Be quiet.' But Beth was scared. Emma had a fistful of CDs – my God, she'd found Conrad's, the ones she'd hidden in her filing cabinet! – and was poised to throw the first. 'And put those down.'

'You'd like that, wouldn't you? You'd like me to be a good little girl. But I'm not. I'm a grown woman, and you've been lying to me.'

'Have I? In what way?' She reviewed possible rooms for a discussion. They were all full of pretty things, all too vulnerable to those CDs. 'Why don't we go into your bedroom and discuss this quietly?'

For answer she got one slicing towards her face. She feinted. The case ricocheted off the front door, smashing. The CD itself spun like a large penny until it sank exhausted on the carpet. Even as she watched, hypnotised, she realised another was on its way. This time there was a yell. The box had struck Bill just above the eyebrow.

There was a lot of blood.

She grabbed him as he staggered and steered him into the kitchen. 'Get a clean tea towel – quick!' she yelled.

Emma whimpered, 'I can't . . . blood . . .'

Grabbing a towel from a drawer, Beth pressed it to Bill's forehead, and eased him on to a chair. Emma for once in her life could wait. Bill groaned, a dreadful shuddering moan.

Emma started to cry.

Bill's groans worsened. Then she saw him wink with the eye further from Emma. She lifted the corner of the tea towel. Given the amount of blood, it was a fairly small puncture. But it would bruise badly – he might even end up with a black eye.

'How are you on butterflies, Bill? There'll be some in my first-aid kit. It's in the bathroom cupboard, Emma. For God's sake pull yourself together and shift yourself.'

If Conrad had been there, she'd have quoted *Pygmalion*. Or was it *My Fair Lady*? He'd have known.

'Collected butterflies all my life,' he said. 'What might also be beneficial is ice, of course. Preferably,' he added, *sotto voce*, 'in a good stiff gin. What I do recommend, however, before you actually touch any of my gore, is that you put on rubber gloves. You never know, Beth, who else has been dabbling in a doctor's blood.'

'Good girl,' she acknowledged as Emma returned, holding the green box at arm's length. 'Now, you see those plastic gloves. Put them on. And then hold this pad to Dr Davis's head while I put gloves on too.'

'I can't . . . I won't . . . I really – no. No. No! NO!' The hysteria got louder and wilder.

Which explained why when Russell and Sylvia came in through the open front door, it was to find a bloodstained elderly man slapping their daughter's face.

'It's amazing,' Bill said, filling the kettle a second time, 'what a decent cup of tea will achieve. I'd still have preferred gin, of course, but I may have to postpone that till after surgery. Are you ready to gird your loins and face them?'

'Have you time to – can you possibly stay for five minutes?' God, what a coward she was being. She'd made Russell and Sylvia take Emma into the living room and had simply delivered a tea tray while they elicited such facts and as much fiction as Emma chose to give them.

She had the excuse, of course, of patching up Bill, but it was an excuse. He could probably have done a

much neater job himself in front of the bathroom mirror.

He was looking at his watch. 'Five minutes is the absolute
maximum. No, hang on. I'll phone to see how may appointments I've got. You never can tell with rain. Sometimes it
seems to make people more aware of their aches and pains;
sometimes it convinces them they should stay in.'

'There's a phone in my study.'

She laid a fresh tray, even – pleased with herself –
remembering a supply of cup-cakes in the freezer. She
microwaved them while she waited for Bill.

'Beth . . .'

'What on earth's the matter?' She almost staggered at the
sight of his serious face.

'I think you should prepare yourself for a bit of a shock.
I think you may have had a burglar. Come upstairs.'

Her study – her lovely study . . .

'See what I mean?'

Books, files, paper, Conrad's CDs – everywhere.

Emma.

'I think her parents should see this while you're here, Bill.
A few sedatives may be in order.' She was shaking so much
she could hardly walk down the stairs.

'What could she have been looking for?'

'Ask her.'

Strange that she hadn't registered a similar problem with
the living room when she'd taken through the tea. Now she
realised why Russell was on his hands and knees. He was
trying to gather and – judging from the tottering piles in
front of him – sort her CDs.

As mildly as she could, she asked, 'What were you
looking for, Emma? Up in my study?'

Emma tore herself from her mother's arms. 'You! Don't
you speak to me! You've been fucking my boyfriend. But
you won't get away with it. I'm going to have his baby!'

Twenty-Three

She mustn't faint. She wouldn't faint. She wasn't the sort of woman to faint. Not a woman like Sylvia, now approaching the sort of hysterics Bill had slapped Emma out of.

Beth took a deep breath, breathed out slowly. Thank God for the self-control honed by all those years' teaching. Thank God for the back of the chair she was holding. 'May one ask when, Emma?'

'None of your business, you old—' More of Gaz's interesting vocabulary.

'But it is. Goodness knows what your parents will think if I allowed you to conceive a child under my roof.'

'He's going to come back and marry me.'

How much longer she could sustain her cool interrogation she'd no idea. 'So it's a putative rather than an actual pregnancy. That's OK, then, isn't it, Sylvia? He's a very nice young man. Let me congratulate you on your new son-in-law. Now, Russell, while Sylvia and Emma discuss the baby's name, I'd like you to step into my study.'

Bill touched her arm. 'I'd best be off. If I have a chance, I'll stop by later. But if I don't, you'll need these.' He pressed two tablets cut from a bubble-pack into her hand.

'Bless you.' She touched his forehead and then leaned to kiss him on the cheek. 'I'm sure I shall be all right.'

'That's what I'm worried about,' he said, plunging into the swirling dusk.

*　　*　　*

182

'You're saying Emma did this? I really can't believe it. No, it's not possible.'

She fished the garage bill from her pocket. 'Sometimes it's easier to believe two impossible things. She'll explain the details. The bill would have been a lot worse only Conrad – the young man in question – insisted on paying for the damage to his car himself. Before you ask, he's a very decent, generous man. What he didn't want Emma to know is what she clearly found out by going through this lot' – she gestured at her wreck of a room – 'that he's a musician. A pop star. He flew to the States yesterday.'

'Leaving my poor little girl on her own – like that! I'll give him flying to the States.'

'No you won't. Because you flew to Italy. And then you went on to Tuscany. And you left Emma with me, knowing I couldn't keep an eye on her. I don't blame you for being a bad parent, Russell. I suspect the vast majority of parents are bad parents. But don't lay any blame on anyone else.'

'Emma's right, isn't she?' came a voice from the door – Sylvia's. 'Beth has been sleeping with poor little Emma's boyfriend. You can hear it in every word she says. Well, what do you expect? A woman who gets engaged to a man who's sleeping with her own pupils. A paedophile.'

Even Russell had the grace to flush. 'No, no. Don't let's bring the Richard business up again. The man's paying his debt, after all.'

'Ten years of debt,' Beth added.

'A decent woman would have stood by him.'

'Cant!' said Beth. Stood by a man she'd loved enough to marry, but who'd subjected her to the humiliation of trial not just in court but also by the media? Well, perhaps she would have done, had it not been for the words he'd thrown at her during her first prison visit. Which were no one's business – no one's but her own. Time for more deep breaths.

'Now, I can hear that rain getting heavier by the minute. And the wind . . . I think you should pack up Emma's things while Russell writes me a cheque. If you don't fancy driving in this lot, Russell – and I can't say I blame you – you'll find an excellent hotel on the road out to Dawlish Warren.'

Russell looked round the room. 'If we helped you tidy up this – well, we could always spend the night on your sofa bed. It wouldn't be the first time.' He smiled ingratiatingly.

Not on the sofa bed. Not the bed Conrad had slept in. Not the bed she'd wanted to seduce him in.

She swallowed hard. They mustn't see her tears, or hear them in her voice. 'I . . .' she began.

Sylvia cut across her. 'The doctor says Emma shouldn't stay on here a moment longer: it was irresponsible of Beth to have her, working at that school with all those germs.'

'Completely irresponsible,' Beth agreed. 'Sylvia's right, Russell. The sooner you get Emma out of my home the better.'

He flinched at the barbed comment. He waited till Sylvia had started down the stairs. 'About the cheque,' he began.

'Oh, don't worry about her food and pocket money,' Beth said, wilfully misunderstanding. 'Aunt's privilege.'

'It's not that as . . . I'm not sure I've got that much in my current account.'

She smiled, sunnily. 'No problem. Give me as much as you can afford now – just so I can pay off my overdraft – and leave me a couple of post-dated cheques. But maybe,' she added, dismayed at the small sum he'd put on the cheque, 'you'd better find a cheaper hotel.'

The sheer pettiness of it. That was what angered her most. Why, Emma had even pulled the mobile-phone charger out of the wall, leaving the phone as it started, battery dead to the world. As for the books – well, no real harm had come to any of them, and at least she could dust them as she slotted them back into their rightful places. She could even make a virtue of sorting out the files as she returned them to the cabinet: why had she kept a pile of bills from her last house? She slung them and other out-of-date papers into a black sack to take eventually to the paper bank.

It occurred to her that there was no reason not to soften the penance – which was, after all, hardly hers – with music. Despite herself, she found herself going downstairs. Maybe, just maybe, those Conrad Tate CDs wouldn't have suffered despite Emma's violence.

She was just fitting the first into the computer when the phone rang.

'Beth. Beth, I've got you at last.'

Conrad himself!

'Are you all right?'

'A couple of problems, nothing much.'

'You're lying,' he said, with tenderness, not rancour. 'Look, I'm not saying this well. Come over. Come over here, now. There. That's what I wanted to say. Please.'

'And destroy Emma? I can't!'

'Sod Emma. She'll get used to it soon enough.'

'And the school – I can't just walk out.'

'It's killing you, woman. Please. Just come.'

'Conrad, I want to, yes, more—'

But the line went dead. He'd cut her off. She'd let him down. Frantic, she jabbed the cradle – he mustn't go. No hum, no whistle, no nothing

Then she realised that the phone really was dead. And she put her head down and cried like a baby.

It must have been hunger that woke her up. It certainly wasn't the sound of the central heating switching on or the radio alarm. The only sounds she could hear were those of the storm still battering the coast. Although the house was two hundred yards from the sea, in the rare intervals of quiet between gusts of wind and the rain's assaults on her windows, she could hear the crash of waves. She reached for the bedside light.

Nothing.

Hell, that was all she needed: a power cut. No heating,

no hot water, no kettle, no toaster. A power cut. Oh, and no light, of course. She'd better feel her way to the candles and matches she kept ready for such an emergency. If only she'd had the sense to buy a paraffin heater when her neighbours had advised her to.

Since there was nothing to keep her at home, she set off for school well before seven. It would be warm and dry there, Jane would rustle up some sort of breakfast, along with reminders of what happened to head teachers who didn't eat, and she could make a start on the paperwork. Her early arrival might also put the fear of God into Bromwich.

How could Conrad have expected her to drop everything and go over? She was needed at the school, wasn't she? It was her job. She was committed to it. All she had to do was get there.

Coast road or over the moor? The main road would be safer, surely. She turned the car inland.

She realised as soon as she picked up the main road from Teignmouth to the A380 that she might have made a bad choice. It wasn't just twigs that littered the road alongside the woodland; it was full-size branches. A Mondeo had already come to grief; the driver was showing the damage to an RAC man. Though she got through to the main road unscathed, there was no whizzing along at seventy. She found herself cowering over the wheel, as if that might somehow lower wind resistance and keep her on the road.

What would it be like at Tucker's Hay? Would that pig be all right?

There was a flurry of flashing lights. She dabbed her emergency lights on and slowed to a halt. A jam already?

A young policeman, bedraggled despite his bright-wear, was picking his way along the cars.

'There's a lorry jackknifed. If you take it gently you might just manage. Or you might try picking up the coast road.' He pointed to a junction. His radio spluttered.

'Cancel that, miss,' he said. 'Floods. They've just closed it.'

If she couldn't get to school, how could she possibly get to Conrad? No, the whole idea was absurd. Heads didn't just take off like that. Think of her diary, not to mention all the other problems today's weather would bring . . .

She herded remnants of classes together and delegated the few teachers who'd battled in to deal with them. She ran to earth some old convector heaters in a stockroom; she organised a phone rota until the phones here went down too. She organised the whole crazy day with the calm efficiency of a woman who dared not stop lest she think of Conrad. Dared not. Dared not.

At one point she borrowed a child's mobile and tried phoning home. No. Dawlish was still cut off, and probably still without power. But it was the only place Conrad would think of reaching her. She had a gas hob, after all. That would warm the kitchen. So she stopped at Sainsbury's, picked up a stir-fry and headed home.

Even with candles it was home. Cold, but home. She might need to sleep dressed and under two duvets, but it was home. She was just collecting the duvet from the sofa bed when she remembered the mobile phone: had that picked up enough charge before the power went off?

Two messages. Both from Conrad. The first was so incoherent she hardly knew what to make of it, except for the word promise. But the second came over loud and clear. His words were unequivocal. 'I love you,' Conrad said.

Twenty-Four

The following morning Beth had no option but to close the school. No light, no heat must mean no staff, no pupils. There was no alternative to closing it. She phoned – Jane's mobile, this time – Christopher Starling, simply, she thought, as a matter of courtesy.

'Are you out of your mind?' he demanded. 'Send the children home if you wish, but you should insist the staff come in. And have the pay stopped of those who don't.'

'Why? There's nothing they can do, even if they can get here. It's not as if most of them can walk in: most depend on public transport.'

'Maybe we should think about that when we make staff appointments in future. Insist that they live within the school's catchment area.'

She was so incensed by his stupid suggestion that she could have lost sight of her original aim. The best thing was to ignore it. 'The current situation is that Exeter is effectively cut off from the south and the west. The sea wall from Dawlish Warren right through to Teignmouth is so battered by the high seas the trains can't use it. The buses replacing the train service can't get through because of floods and fallen trees.'

'You got in.'

'Christopher, a quarter of the staff got through yesterday, a tenth of the children.'

'The staff should have meetings,' he insisted. 'And get on with marking and preparation.'

'If you want the school to be the subject of a complaint to

the Health and Safety Executive, that's fine,' she said. 'The average temperature in the school yesterday afternoon was fifty-four. No one should work in such conditions – not if we want them to come in fit and healthy when power is restored.'

'You're clearly determined to have your own way. But rest assured, I shall raise the matter at the next governors' meeting.' He rang off.

She passed the phone back to Jane, whose eyes couldn't have been much wider. Cancelling Friday's dinner was only a matter of gamesmanship, wasn't it? Who could hold out longer?

Meanwhile, there was the important matter of Jane's date with David Keane.

'How did it go last night?'

Jane grimaced. 'It didn't. David was working. He phoned – oh, grovelled. And postponed it till tonight. He sent you a message, by the way.' Jane peered at Beth's feet. 'That's odd. You've got lovely straight toes! But he said something about bunions being catching.'

Which was how Beth spent the afternoon in much warmer conditions than she'd expected. As she was locking up at around midday, David Keane put his head round the door. 'I wanted to discuss our big toes,' he said. 'But Jane's right – it's an ice-box in here. It makes it look a bit formal, but would you rather come back to the police station and talk there? We've still got electricity there.'

'Sure. If you don't mind stopping off for me to get a sandwich from somewhere, that'd be fine.'

This time he looked at his watch openly. 'I suppose it must be lunchtime. Why don't the three of us find a pub somewhere? A nice warm one.'

'Why should Jeff remove all the tapes?' David asked, an hour later. They were in an anonymous grey interview room.

'Don't be threatened by this,' David had said, gesturing at the tape recorder. 'I know it's where we interview suspects. But my office is being painted and the smell gives me splitting headaches.'

'Fine by me.' Except that it wasn't. Not really. Not after the Richard business, and all those agonising hours being interviewed. Would she ever get over that?

Her voice must have given her away. He looked hard at her, but obviously decided not to press her. 'How would he benefit by closing down your security system?'

'Who knows? Have you asked him?'

'He insists it's on your orders. I didn't believe him,' he added, with the sort of smile that must have turned Jane's heart. 'I think it might be on someone else's. Tell me, Beth, all about your relationship with Mr Starling.'

It had been nearly five when she'd left the police station. As the wind and rain swirled into her face, she knew she couldn't face the prospect of a difficult drive home to an icy house. Even if her bank account were empty, she could still use her credit card. Exeter abounded in hotels and guest houses: she'd buy herself a change of clothes and book in to one of them.

The clothes buying was easy: finding a hotel less so. The road and rail situation, of course. But Tourist Information found her a clean, neat guest house at last. She charged her mobile, but couldn't get back to Conrad. At least she could leave a message. What sort of message would a competent, articulate, highly paid career woman leave? A hesitant, stumbling one. But she managed, she thought, to say the important things: that she loved him, that she wished she could have been with him, that she wished him everything wonderful for his concert tonight. Most of all, yes, that she loved him.

Her room didn't run to satellite TV, alas, so she wouldn't be able to see his concert, but it did run to an en suite bathroom and she felt she'd earned a luxurious soak before she had to turn out and get a meal. The soak, and the Channel Four News headlines.

The storm damage was even worse than she could have imagined. The whole of the south was in trouble, the gale-force winds whipping up high tides to penetrate coastal defences. Trees across roads and railway lines were causing travel havoc, compounded by a medium-size plane being blown across a runway at Heathrow. Manchester and Birmingham Airports were overwhelmed with redirected flights. Cross-channel sailings had been suspended. She managed a bleak smile: hadn't there once been a newspaper headline declaring that with fog in the Channel, Europe was cut off?

This was no good. If she didn't go out now, all the restaurants would be full. It was bad enough – yes, it probably always would be bad enough – to be a woman on her own, but to compete with couples for a rare table would be to set herself up as a hungry loser. On with the soaking raincoat.

There was a tap at the door. Her landlady, asking if she fancied taking pot luck with her family: it turned out her daughter was at King's Barton. Well, if the penalty for eating in was a stilted conversation with a pupil, that seemed minor compared with having to turn out into the elements, so Beth accepted gladly. And then came the nice surprise. The food was not only excellent – a home-made vegetable soup, herb-flavoured chicken joints with baked potatoes and vegetables, and baked apples – it was prepared by Helena, the pupil herself. The parents produced a couple of bottles of good Italian wine, on the house, they insisted, so they sat round, listening to the rain slapping against the windows and gossiped like old friends. The nicest surprise of all was that Helena didn't want to cook for a career: no, she rather thought she'd like to be a nuclear physicist. If only they could improve the pay-scales for government scientists.

Fed and watered, Beth fell into bed. She knew Conrad loved her; he only had to play back his messages to know

she loved him. Tomorrow, surely they'd be able to talk ear
to ear, not answerphone to answerphone. She slept long and
dreamlessly.

However well they'd got on the evening before, Beth
thought it might embarrass Helena to have to walk into
school with her.

'It's highly likely we'll be closed again. If we're not, I'll
phone your mother,' she said.

The rain was certainly much lighter, and she fancied the
wind had dropped. In fact, when she parked at school, the
weather felt exhilarating rather than terrifying. Perhaps
the worst was past and life would soon return to normal.
The newsagent opposite the school shared her optimism.
He was already carrying out his display boards. She
scanned the headlines on the first:

POPSTAR IN U.S. COLLAPSE

Twenty-Five

From a long way away, Beth saw herself walk carefully across the road into the newsagent's, pick up two papers – a broadsheet and a red-top – pay, counting out the exact change, and walk into school. She was so cold she thought she'd never stop shaking. The *Guardian* probably wouldn't even have run the story – when she saw it wasn't on the front page, she gave up and turned to the *Mirror*. Plenty in there. A photo of him huddled on the stage. More inside, no doubt from the files, with photos of women with whom his name had been linked in the past. There was a lot of gossip about his past – wild times when he'd conned the Prime Minister's Office into believing he was a visiting overseas dignitary, when he'd turned the tables on a patronising TV interviewer by persuading someone to substitute footage of the windbag, not himself, in a peak-time programme. Other, less harmless jokes – though most of those seemed to be very much in the past. Not much actual news, but enough. Conrad Tate had been stretchered offstage after the last number of his farewell concert. Hands raised to acknowledge the ecstatic applause, he'd suddenly grabbed his left arm and tumbled forward. At first it was feared some crazed fan had shot him; now it seemed more likely he'd had a heart attack. He'd been rushed to a private clinic.

Beth was amazed how calm she was. She didn't even rush to the staff loo. Just walked there quietly, and without fuss lost her breakfast.

And then walked calmly back again. She had to get to him. However remote the chance of getting a flight to

New York, she would get one. The earliest. From wherever.

The Internet. They said that was the best way to get tickets. The Internet meant a computer and it meant electricity or a charged battery and a live phone line.

In Exeter?

Where on earth could she find one in Exeter?

Not at the school. No power, no phones.

Why in God's name had she never got round to organising it at home? Why for God's sake had she always postponed . . .

But she was being stupid. No phone, no electricity in Dawlish. So even if she had . . .

So where?

She looked at her watch. She'd wasted a minute already. Think, woman, think! Everything depended on her shutting down her emotions and using her head. Think: where would there be power and phones and computers?

David Keane's laugh was very kind. 'It's usually people who help us with our enquiries! But of course I'll help you with yours.' He put a hand on her arm as he steered her out of the police station. 'You can use the computer at my place. Leave your car where it is. I'll run you there and then bring you back.'

She knew that as he drove he glanced at her from time to time, but she couldn't think of anything to say or do. She found he was holding her elbow as he led her up the short path to his house. How dared he hold her as if she were a shaky old lady? But her legs insisted they didn't want to support her, so she was silent and grateful.

'Let me make you a cup of tea first,' he said.

She wanted to scream at him for even thinking about wasting a moment. She mustn't. He was being kind. She was getting hysterical. She must keep calm. 'But—'

He patted her shoulder. 'OK, maybe it would be better if I got on with the biz with the Internet. You make the cup of tea. And drink it. You'll find plenty of sugar in the bag in the left-hand cupboard. Beth – remember to put plenty of sugar in your tea.'

What use would she be to Conrad if she couldn't even register where she was? She tried to concentrate. If she thought about the detail of David's kitchen, maybe she wouldn't worry why he was taking so long. So she looked at the notes on his cork-board, at the tea stains on the table cloth, at the newly cleaned litter tray and at the washing chugging round in the machine and just about to spin. A nice domesticated kitchen. What was Conrad's like? Would she ever see it now?

She could bear it no longer. Picking up both mugs she set off to find him.

'Up here! In the back bedroom.'

She hadn't even realised it was an old house till her shoes rung out on the tiles of the hall floor. Yes, high ceilings, plasterwork on the cornices. Was it David who'd restored it?

'There are several places on a flight from Dublin first thing tomorrow.'

'Yes!'

'Just one problem, remember, Beth: we can't get you to Dublin. The Irish Sea sailings are all suspended.'

'Flights?'

'All those shoals of people wanting to get back to the States. And the log-jams at the major airports . . .' He shrugged.

'What do I do?' Damn and damn, she sounded as helpless at Emma on a bad day.

'I could get you a ticket club class for tomorrow evening from Heathrow. Provided the airport's back to normal. That's your best bet.'

'Tomorrow evening. He might be dead by then.' Dead, not knowing she loved him enough to give up everything.

'Stop it. You're being melodramatic. He's in the States, remember. With a wallet the size of Texas, from what the papers say. Come on, he won't be hanging round all day on a trolley in A and E. He'll get the best, Beth. The best in the world.'

She nodded. Giving up everything . . . What was she giving up? Nothing at all, not really. What did she care about the approval of the governors? At worst, she might lose a job she no longer wanted. So why had she hesitated? Common sense, of course. She'd known him days, that was all. Days. He'd been kind to her. Sensible. Friendly. Was that a basis for lifelong love?

How could it be? But that wasn't what Conrad had asked her for. All he'd asked for was a grand gesture. He'd not offered to set her free: he'd offered her the opportunity to do that for herself. If she'd failed that test, she couldn't fail the next. She could do it for him. 'Headmistress abandons school to be with pop star' – she could see the headlines already. Except they'd be pithier than that. Cruder.

'Have you got your credit card there?' David asked. 'And I can book your train ticket too.'

David hadn't been happy about letting her drive back to Dawlish on her own. But she'd insisted, and since the rain had almost stopped when she picked up her car, he gave way.

'I still think you should ask Jane to be with you.' His face softened as he said the name.

For the first time that day, she managed a smile. 'She's such a good woman it's all too easy to impose on her. I do it enough at school. I can't do it on a bonus day off. She'll have enough to do when I flit off.'

'You won't be going back, will you?' There was surprisingly little judgement in his voice.

'I may have to. I can't just leave them in the lurch. But that's one of the things I shall be doing today. Writing my letter of resignation to the LEA. Copy to Christopher Starling.'

He looked at her sideways. 'Always assuming he'll still be chair of your governors.'

'Is there any doubt?'

'Have you got two minutes?' She nodded, but stayed where she was. He could update her in the car park as well as anywhere. He seemed content. 'If anyone asks, I've not said this. Well, according to your predecessor, he'd shown very little interest in her till the Christmas in her second year, though she'd always felt able to rely on his judgement and advice. Then they had – her words, not mine – a whirlwind romance.'

She dredged through her memory. 'They sold the playing fields in March, didn't they?'

'And their relationship ended in April. It has to be said she saw nothing sinister at all in what had happened.'

'Does she still carry a torch for him? Women my age – we can find it hard to shake from our hearts the most unsuitable men. You know doubt know all about me and Richard Palmer.'

He nodded. 'I'm glad you're not involved with Starling. My feet are playing up something shocking,' he added with a grin. Then his face became grim. 'I don't know why Bromwich should have nicked those videos – but I should imagine we'll find out today. Maybe a rebuilding contract . . .'

No light. No heat. But at least the house had suffered no damage. The garden was littered with branches, and tiles from her neighbour's roof. A couple of her pots had been smashed by one or another. She scooped the shards into the bin. She must remember to leave it at the bottom of the drive for whenever the bin-men came. Maybe she'd already missed them. For the life of her she couldn't remember which day they came. Even which day today was. Well, it would be ready whenever they came. And that must be the theme of the day. She must shut down the house, put it to bed. Everything from houseplants to the contents of her vegetable rack. And what should she take with her? Clothes for how long? Remembering, of course, that while New York didn't lack for shops, her credit card wasn't bottomless, her account was quite empty, and that she'd no longer have a salary coming in.

And there was the school. She'd better apply herself to making detailed notes for whoever took over in her absence. God! Was she really doing this? Abandoning all those children, all those adults? For love? For no more than the potential for love?

For answer she got out her passport and case and started to pack.

She was so cold she could have cursed David for booking her a ticket for the morning: it would have made more sense to set off tonight and stay at an airport hotel overnight. Then she remembered what he'd said about the chaos. No, he'd done the best he could. And by now, surely they couldn't be far from restoring power. And the phone. At least she'd managed to get enough charge into her mobile now. It was good not to be incommunicado. Except, of course, that most of her friends and neighbours still were. Swathing herself in both an old sleeping bag and a duvet, she settled down to write notes to them all.

There. A pile to post. All stamped, ready, from the big envelope for the school to a set of notelets meant to sound apologetic but to her eyes and ears ringing with love. 'Visiting a sick friend . . . Not sure when I'll be back . . .'

Setting both alarm clocks and her mobile phone – she was sure she wouldn't sleep but couldn't risk dropping into a deep dawn sleep – she huddled into bed at about midnight. At fifteen minutes past, the bedside light came on. She felt as grateful as if the poor men working out there had been exposed to the wind and the rain just for her. She'd been cold, but their fingers must have been numb with cold, slippery with rain. She must remember them in her prayers, alongside those in peril on the sea. And those in whatever hospital, wherever. Especially those.

No. She shouldn't even have hoped for sleep.

On impulse, she reached for her mobile, just to hear the sound of his voice. Yes, there were his messages. *Remember your promise. I love you.*

Her promise? Not to believe anything that she heard through the media?

No, none of it made sense.

Twenty-Six

A nd it made even less sense that she was dancing in her own study, just as she'd danced before. In Conrad's arms.

'I just got straight on a plane,' he was saying. 'Soon as the gig was over. The problem was getting into Heathrow. They had to land at Schipol eventually. Then I got a plane to Glasgow. And a train that went via everywhere.'

She pushed away from him – all that pain! 'You should have phoned. You've no idea what . . . Was it meant to be a joke? One of your dreadful jokes?'

'Please – please look at me. In my head it might have started out as one. And Joe Public may still think it was. There's a press release ready and waiting to go out, incidentally, saying I'm going to make a complete recovery but need absolute quiet and privacy. Everything will have blown over in a week: I'm not a major player in the music world any more. But it really wasn't a joke. I . . . Beth, I had to think of something that would . . . Look, you'd always have put the school and duty first, wouldn't you? Or worried about Emma. Or worried – oh, about God knows what. But this way – I thought it'd force you to make a decision. And' – he pointed to her case – 'it did, didn't it?'

'That's no excuse!' She bit back tears and took deep breaths. 'Yes, to be honest, I suppose it is, isn't it? Just about. But – oh, Conrad – why on earth didn't you phone?'

Almost in tears himself, he clasped her hands. 'I tried. Beth, my love, I tried. Here. The school. Your mobile. Everything dead. In the end it just seemed easier to come

200

here. This was where I wanted to be, after all. With you,' he added, relinquishing one hand so that he could touch her face.

She couldn't speak.

He pushed back her hair. 'Can you ever forgive me?'

Could she? Could she ever forget the agony he'd put her through, even if she forgave him? She swallowed. 'How did you get in?' It was easier to ask practical questions.

'I copied the keys you lent Emma. She *has* gone?'

'Oh yes. Not before, I'm afraid, she'd found out who you were – she broke into my filing cabinet and found the CDs I'd hidden there. And almost certainly stuff about my past I should have told you about.'

He bent to kiss her. 'Don't you think I remember the case? My poor Beth.'

The lights dipped, flickered back on and then went out altogether.

'That settles it,' he said, his hold tightening. 'We go to Tucker's Hay. Log fires and candles – and a generator if they pall.'

'But—'

'All those preparations you've made – all those letters piled by the front door. Including that fat envelope for school. Farewell notes, I'd say! No one will expect to see you for – how long?'

She shook her head helplessly. Not that he'd see.

'We have to talk, sweetheart. Not just my future but yours. And I've got a plan – oh, something very vague just yet – about getting deprived kids into musical education. I'd like your views on that. Views, and help. Come with me. Please.'

'The school . . .'

'What if you'd got a promotion somewhere else? Couldn't they replace you? Well, then – work out your notice. With someone at hand to love and cherish you – hell, if you give me that cook-book you promised me, I'll have your meal waiting on the table for you.'

'Sounds wonderful.' At last her face remembered how to smile.

'You may have to give me a few lessons first. But I reckon you're a good teacher – and I'll try to be an apt pupil. Beth, come with me.'

The clouds must have shifted, but she didn't need the pale light from the stars, a glimmer from the moon to know how much he wanted her. Nor how much she wanted him.

But he didn't want their first time to be here, cluttered as it was with memories of Emma and her machinations. Horribly aware that he'd said something similar before, he said, 'I want our first time to be special. Not a clinging together in the cold. Come with me now. You've got your car. Get some clothes on while I load it. And we'll post those letters at the first pillar box. Buy ourselves a little time.'

She wanted to agree. He knew she did. He sought desperately for some clinching argument. He held back a smile. 'You may need someone wise to talk everything over with. And I know just the person. Beth – come with me to Tucker's Hay and meet Falstaff.'

And she slipped her hand into his and led him down the stairs.